VEGAS BABY

A STEAMY CONTEMPORARY HOLIDAY ROMANCE

PERRY HARBOR

BOOK 4.5

CHRISTINA BRAVER

Cover by: Design Wheel Graphics
Edited by: Lynne Pearson, All That Editing, Inc.
ISBN: 979-8-9885479-0-7 (ebook) 979-8-9885479-1-4 (print)

Find the author:
Facebook - @christinabraverromance
Instagram - christinabraverromance
Visit the author's website at www.christinabraver.com

1

HANNAH

"Yes! Right there ... don't stop." I wasn't above begging.

Lorenzo met my demand with grunts and thrusts as he pressed me against the wall, his lean, hard body moving in a relentless rhythm. The raw, animal sound was a contradiction to his smooth honey skin and pillowy, full lips teasing along my jaw between kisses. We were both still mostly dressed, and the hard points of my nipples grazed against my fine lace bra, sending delicious jolts straight to my core. My panties were soaked, had been for hours, and my sex-deprived body ached.

One night. A fantasy come to life. And it had been so long since I indulged in anything this exciting and reckless.

In a rush, the build and tension reached a breaking point. "I'm coming," I panted as the wave of pleasure crashed over me.

"Yes!" Lorenzo shouted, his warm Italian accent filling the cavernous suite as he joined me.

I loved orgasms. They were the great equalizer. Rich or poor, orgasms didn't care. They felt just as good in a

$2,000-per-night French hotel room as they did in my simple and comfortable one-bedroom loft in Oregon. Not that there had been many orgasms in my loft with anyone other than my trusty vibe.

My head was fuzzy from alcohol and travel, but I logged every touch and sensation in my memory. Lorenzo Messina was the former Formula Two racing-phenom who rose out of the amateur ranks to be the newest driver on the Formula One field, replacing Walker Hewitt, who retired after last season. Team Jaguar was in good hands if Lorenzo could drive for the checkered flag as well as he drove for my orgasm.

Much younger, brazen, and flirty with bright baby blues, he'd been my favorite naughty fantasy for months. Regarded as the best new driver this year, Lorenzo was just getting started. He had a full life ahead of him that did not include a committed relationship with a straightforward statistics professor, no matter who my family was. We were just having a bit of summer holiday fun surrounded by the classical opulence of the Cheval Blanc Paris.

Luxury fabric in a subtle shade of taupe. White gossamer curtains blowing in the warm evening breeze scented with flowers. Iron-framed glass doors open to the top floor balcony and a view of the Pont Neuf bridge, the Seine, and the twinkling lights of Paris in summer. It was my favorite hotel in France, probably in all of Europe.

I'd shared a love of Formula One with my father since I could say *vroom*. Whenever my family was in Europe for a grand prix, we always stopped in Paris to relax for a few days. Parisians either didn't recognize my parents or didn't care. This made it one of our favorite spots for vacation.

There hadn't been a French Grand Prix this year, the organizers blaming politics. But it was money. Everything always came down to money. And with France off the official calendar, several F1 teams had started their mid-season break in the City of Lights.

After attending the Belgian Grand Prix with my father, I'd taken a few extra days for a solo trip here as well. I wasn't too shocked to find my favorite naughty fantasy sitting in the hotel bar like he was waiting for me.

"Mi fai impazzire. That was incredible," Lorenzo said, lowering my legs of jelly to the floor and tucking away his still half-hard dick. We weren't done.

He pressed me again to the textured velvet wall covering as he bent to nip my bare shoulder. I was wearing my iconic, aqua-blue, Halston halter dress with an asymmetrical hem. The silky satin wrapped around my upper body and neck so magically that it made my smallish breasts look fantastic. Lorenzo's hands were back underneath the skirt, stroking the bare skin at my hips and making it hard for me to translate his words, but I think he said I drove him crazy. "No more making love to women my age," he whispered against my neck. "Mature women know what they are doing. Sei la donna dei miei sogni."

I scoffed. "First, do not call the 'woman of your dreams' mature unless she's eighty." I smacked his chest playfully but didn't move away. I was thirty. Not quite Mrs. Robinson. "Second, there's no need to lay it on so thick. I wanted this as much as you did."

At twenty-one, Lorenzo had grinned like a natural-born seducer living on top of the world. And I'd enjoyed being with him there, and against the wall, and in the soft bed for those sweet, sexy hours in Paris. Hook up with an F1 driver? Check that off my bucket list.

"Professor Byrne? Hannah!"

Blinking out of my months-old memory, three months to be exact, I startled and peered over my shoulder to find my colleague, Professor Grant Robolin. He stood behind me in the faculty kitchen of the sciences and engineering building at Oregon Pacific University, a smallish private university outside Bend. Giving my head one more shake, I pushed past the vibrant memories.

Older and frustrating, Grant was everything Lorenzo wasn't.

Wearing his standard faded blue jeans with a funky blazer over a crisp white button-up and a simple navy tie, all he needed was to stand among the October color outside, and he'd be a GQ-worthy advertisement for this place. He looked edible, unfortunately. Why were the bad ones always so hot?

He smelled of soap and aftershave. Something earthy with sweet, subtle notes like whiskey. The ends of his dark hair, cut close and peppered with gray at the edges, were damp, likely from his usual after-workout shower.

As an adjunct professor, Grant taught practicum classes three days a week in the physical therapy department housed here in the same building as the math department and several others. He was smart and confident, and he made me crazy. Not in a good way. Well, sometimes in a good way, but that was only in my crazy fantasies late at night. In real life, he was a pain in my butt.

The thermostat for our adjacent offices was in his. Since he took up residence in that space last year, shortly after he was hired, he adjusted the temperature to his liking and expected *me* to accommodate it. Typical male.

For those first few months, I thought he was trying to freeze me to death in some evil plan to return the divided space to its original super-sized corner office just for him. Then I realized he was *trying* to irritate me. He seemed to enjoy it. Again, typical juvenile male, though every bit of him appeared to be a full-grown man.

"Can't find your lunch?" Grant asked.

"What?" I squinted at him, still a little dazed.

"You've been standing in front of an open refrigerator for over a minute. If you haven't found what you're looking for, it's likely not in there. Or were you frozen from the cold air inside?" He winked.

Normally, I'd respond to his teasing barb, but I hadn't felt normal in … well, four days and about seven hours.

"Oh, right." I stood to my full height and closed the door. "I was looking for the leftover soup from the fall faculty pot-luck last night. Meredith said she left some in here."

My eyes landed on the dishes in Grant's hand, two of which looked very much like empty soup containers. I snapped my gaze to his in question.

He shrugged a shoulder. "These were the only two that I saw."

"And you took them both?" I put my hand on my hip, incredulous.

"I was hungry."

"You didn't think someone else might want one?" My lips formed a thin line as I raised my brows.

"They weren't marked, and it was close to one o'clock." He checked the sporty watch on his wrist. "I figured if someone wanted it, they would have taken it already."

I sighed. "Guess I'm off to the Union then." The snack bar inside the student union was only marginally better than your average snack kiosk at the airport, but it was the closest option. I had office hours starting in twenty minutes.

The thought of food had my stomach sinking. Suddenly, my mouth watered, and I felt the familiar sickness rising. I pressed my hand to my head and took a deep breath. I needed to eat.

Grant walked to the trash and recycling bins next to the refrigerator. He brushed his hands together as if he were dusting off crumbs and strolled back to me, bringing his intoxicating scent with him.

"How about this? I know you have office hours soon, so I'll run to Harpers and see what soup they have."

I brushed my hand over my middle. I wanted to argue, but that was too sweet of a deal. "That would be very nice of you."

He shrugged. "I'll grab a sandwich for myself. Today was cardio, and I added an extra mile to my run. I'm still a little hungry."

Of course his good deed would benefit him too. But I wasn't going to complain. Harpers Dining Hall food was much better than the snack kiosk.

2

GRANT

Something was off. It wasn't like Hannah to be staring into the refrigerator. She was usually single-minded and driven. Ready with a quip or succinct chastisement if I did something to agitate her. Which I tried to do as often as reasonably possible. I wasn't a dick, but I did enjoy seeing that spark in her eyes.

God, she was sexy. Toned legs, perfect small breasts that bounced a little when she stomped toward me, crystal blue eyes and dark red hair cut short. And thousands, maybe millions of freckles. I wanted to count them, press my lips to each one, going lower to discover if they were everywhere or only on the skin exposed to the sun.

I'd wanted to know the answer to that question since the first time she barged into my office a little over a year ago. I'd only been on campus a handful of times before that, ordering supplies for my first year as a part-time professor and building a set of cedar shelves. My office had the thermostat for both of our spaces, and she asked me to turn on the heat. It was August.

Struck by the sight of her, it took me a minute to process the request.

I'd obliged but shut it off when I thought she was gone for the day. I'd stripped down to my T-shirt to keep from sweating through my navy button-up before my first evening class when she appeared to confront me about the now cooler office temp. Her blue eyes blazed dark with irritation.

I fucking loved it. At that moment, I promised to battle with her over the thermostat and anything else if it meant seeing that color of blue set against her skin, dotted with freckles like a Seurat masterpiece.

Bringing back that blaze in any other way was not an option. I didn't date people I worked with, especially those in the same building. I'd done that once to disastrous results and learned from my mistake. A relationship wouldn't last, and when it ended, I didn't want one or both of us avoiding the other when we were supposed to be molding the young doctors and scientists of the future.

That didn't mean I hadn't considered breaking that rule with Hannah. The idea pulsed at the edges almost daily.

I hadn't intended to eat the soup she wanted. Again, not a dick. But I could buy her a decent lunch. We were colleagues. Acquaintances. Not close friends, but not enemies.

The walk to the dining hall on the other side of campus was pleasant in the autumn sunshine. The fake cobwebs with giant spiders crawling over them on the side of the administration building were my favorite of the Halloween decorations popping up around campus.

With the lunch rush over, the place wasn't crowded. Checking the soup selections, I hit the jackpot. Poblano corn chowder was Hannah's favorite. I'd heard her tell

Meredith, the math department administrative assistant, multiple times.

I selected a large to-go container and ladled a generous amount of the spicy soup inside. If there was extra, she could eat it for dinner. Considering the sides, I grabbed another compostable take-out container, added a salad similar to the ones I'd seen Hannah make for herself at the occasional faculty lunch or dinner, and snagged a wedge of cornbread just in case. Selecting a decent, ready-made turkey club for myself, I headed to the register to pay.

Back at our building, I climbed the sleek floating staircase from the open lobby to the second floor and found Hannah's office door open. A small space heater whirred in the corner, and I took a moment just to look at her. She looked tired today.

"Hey, lunch," I said, hefting the bag in demonstration.

She glanced up from her laptop. "That was fast." Standing, she shifted one stack of books on top of another, and I placed the bag in the empty spot.

"They had your favorite."

Her eyes glittered, and she opened the bag to take a sniff. "Poblano chowder and a side of cornbread? How did you know?" She removed the contents, stacked my sandwich on top of the salad, and handed both to me.

"The salad is yours too."

"You bought me both the cornbread *and* the salad?"

"I've seen you eat both and didn't know which you'd prefer today."

She blinked a few times. "Thank you. That was very … nice of you." Her eyes softened, and she swallowed. "Do you … the least I can do is invite you to sit and eat your sandwich. I don't have anyone signed up for a meeting right now."

My heart thumped. I wanted to, but I didn't date

coworkers. I know she was only offering lunch, but then I'd want dinner and talking and a helluva lot more after that.

Instead, I stuck to my usual story. "I would, but it's like an oven in here." I loosened my tie dramatically. She said nothing as she sat and continued to set up her lunch. Not typical.

"Hey, is everything okay?" I lowered my voice.

"Sure, what do you mean?" She straightened and pulled her shoulders back.

"Nothing, just staring into the fridge earlier and now, well …"

She sucked in a breath and smoothed a lock of hair from her forehead. "I'm fine. Thank you. I … have a lot on my mind right now, but everything's fine."

"Anything I can do to help?" I asked with a tone that let her know I meant it.

"No, thank you." Her expression was soft, resigned.

I gave her a single head nod. "Okay then." I turned to find a student darkening Hannah's door. "It looks like you have an appointment after all. I'll leave you to it."

3

HANNAH

"Hannah, pay attention," my younger sister, Bethany, snapped. "We're in Vegas. Security is important here."

I huffed a laugh. "I think Hud's speech is mostly for your friends." I turned to Emily, Jo, and Tess, three women who'd joined Bethany for a pre-Thanksgiving girls' trip the same November weekend I was staying in our family's luxe penthouse in the Wynn Hotel for a little getaway of my own.

The Las Vegas Grand Prix was the first F1 race here since 1982, and for a couple of reasons, I didn't want to miss it. Already, the air crackled with excitement beyond the usual colorful flashing lights and overwhelming Vegas kitsch.

My father and I hadn't been to any events since Belgium, and I'd planned to be on my own for this one. I was here to watch, but mostly I was here to meet with Lorenzo. We needed to talk about what happened in Paris.

Hud, short for Hudson, was my family's longtime head of security and was uncompromising with our safety. My father, the now famous Mike Rhodes, together with former

F1 driver Walker Hewitt's father, started Hewitt Computer Company decades ago. It became a global leader in computer manufacturing, and with that success came wealth and notoriety requiring highly professional personal security. Particularly after Bethany and I were born.

Hud and his team had been as much a part of my life as my shadow, always blending into the surroundings. You wouldn't have known they were there if you hadn't assumed we had a security detail. Occasionally, I even forgot, and for those wonderful moments, I was a normal kid like everyone else.

A host of tech professionals and lawyers kept mine and Bethany's faces out of the media until well past each of our eighteenth birthdays. The public knew we existed, but outside of our personal worlds of school and activities, most people couldn't have picked us out of a line-up.

As adults, that anonymity paid off. Neither of us wanted bodyguards around the clock. We lived our lives, went to work, went out with friends. Usually, we were monitored remotely using a highly specialized chip in our phones and watches. In situations deemed riskier, like a girls' weekend in Vegas during an F1 race, on-site personnel under Hud's supervision were brought in for additional support. In spite of all that, we did our best to live normal lives.

Standing at the floor-to-ceiling windows overlooking the Strip already bursting with holiday decorations among the F1 ads, I tried to listen to Hud's speech on emergency protocols.

"This is Anka Petrovsky. Her team will be providing your security." Hud glanced at the nods from Bethany and her friends. Tonight, they were headed to an early show and dinner at the latest Top Chef restaurant in the hotel.

Hud gave me a nod. "I'll be with you." I grinned as

calm settled over me. Knowing I'd have his familiar presence for the weekend, not just at the Formula One VIP meet-and-greet today, was comforting.

I DRESSED CONSERVATIVELY for the late-afternoon event. An ecru sleeveless shirtdress by Dior with black buttons running down the length of the center and a multi-color design of flowers and tree limbs artfully covering one side. This was not about sex. Well, not about having sex.

We passed event security and entered the grand ballroom with its tall windows facing the street. The race was days away, but the crowd had already started forming. As usual, Hud faded to the background with all the other private personnel after a reminder of our *safety phrase* to be used if he had to contact me by phone. It was old school, but it worked.

I joined a group of friends I knew from past racing events. Cheek kissing and listening intently to the next outrageous engagement or world-travel story as crystal glasses clinked in the background was an oddly familiar and comforting pattern.

"May I bring you a drink, ladies?" A waiter, resembling a *Magic Mike* extra, appeared with a twinkle in his eye.

The others ordered bespoke cocktails or white wine.

"Soda water and lime for me," I said.

"At least have him slip a little vodka in there," said Alice Lamaster, heir to the Lamaster Performance Tires fortune.

Magic Mike turned to me with his eyebrows raised. "No, no, thank you. I've had a couple of drinks already and need to pace myself," I lied. Alice nudged me with a wink and a smile.

The crowd buzzed as the drivers began to trickle in.

One at a time, they headed to appointed spots under promotional banners. The sound of cooing young women was distinct, and I craned my neck to see the Team Jag area. Lorenzo smiled like the panty melter he was and waved as flashes from raised cell phones exploded.

He was a star on the rise.

"God, he's gorgeous," Alice said under her breath. "I heard you two had dinner in Paris a few months ago." She raised her eyebrows at me. I said nothing, and she continued, lowering her voice. "Well, if you want a little more than dinner this time, you may have missed your chance with the young one. We all may have. He's rumored to be spending a lot of time with some British actress. A former child-star or something." She sighed. "Damn actresses. They always get the good ones." Flipping her glossy black hair over her shoulder, she glanced around the room.

I kept my expression even. I hadn't heard about a girlfriend. It could be a publicity stunt. He wouldn't be the first new driver to gain broader recognition by dating someone already famous. But if it were true, it was good news and would probably make getting what I wanted easier.

Our eyes met, and that star-wattage smile fell on me. Lorenzo and I weren't a thing, far from it, but he was still swoony perfection. Images of our evening in Paris flashed in my mind making me smile back.

Dating and relationships were difficult in my world. Because of my father's wealth and our family name, I was a target. Trusting people was challenging and happily-ever-after nearly impossible despite how desperately I'd tried to make it happen when I was younger. An occasional one-night stand was simpler, more pragmatic. Lorenzo had his own need for caution and discretion, which had made our particular liaison easy.

Sleeping with an F1 superstar had been an impulse, but I didn't regret it. I soaked in the glow of his charm. It wouldn't last. Girlfriend or not, I wasn't at this party to land another hookup. I'd come to tell him I was pregnant, and he was the father.

4

GRANT

"Dr. Robolin." The energetic female voices stopped me.

I sighed and turned to see two eager young women moving closer across the grand hotel lobby. I wasn't a doctor. At forty, it had been twenty years since I applied to PT school, and professional training had stopped with a master's. Now, most physical therapy programs were doctoral programs. I'd been working in the field for more than fifteen years, and I wasn't going back to college just for more letters after my name.

"Grant. Call me Grant." I smiled wanly and stuck out my hand. It had been a long day, and I was tired from lecturing at two back-to-back sessions for the American Association of Physical Therapists' Annual Sports Symposium. The distant ringing from the casino and the slight hint of air freshener meant to cover the cigarette smoke added to my fatigue and low-grade headache.

"Hi, I'm Casey." She shook my hand, then held it a beat longer, her gaze intent, before releasing me. "And this is Kinsey." She gestured to her friend dressed in tight jeans, a buttoned-up, double-breasted suit jacket, and what looked like nothing underneath. I recognized them both as enthusiastic participants in my lectures.

"We wanted to let you know how much we enjoyed your sessions. We think your ideas about the mobility deficits of athletes in gear are revolutionary." She batted her lashes and moved close enough for me to see down the deep V of the silky top she wore with funky patterned suit pants and a matching jacket.

Hardly revolutionary, I'd simplified guidelines for training athletes to safely compensate for mobility loss when in uniform, like from high-top cleats that limited movement. The body would compensate for the lost flexibility in other ways, and if we trained the muscles to compensate in healthy ways, some on-field injuries could be decreased by as much as half.

The other one, Kinsey or Kelly, tossed her long blonde hair over her shoulder. "We'd love to talk with you more. Over a drink?" Her eyes glittered with suggestion. "Since the conference ends tomorrow, this may be our last … opportunity to meet with you together, just the *three* of us." She bit her bottom lip and stared at my mouth.

"Oh …" I paused, stalling. A three-way offer? Fucking Vegas. You didn't *have* to go wild just because you could.

The girls couldn't be much older than my students. Standing close with that obvious provocative expression on their faces was not a good look for me. I searched the huge lobby area of the Wynn Hotel's exhibition hall as if the answer to *how to get out of this easily* would be written on the walls.

At that moment, a miracle happened. Hannah appeared in my line of sight. What was she doing here?

I blinked to face Callie or Casey or Cassie and her friend. "I'm sorry. I have plans with my girlfriend." I gestured toward Hannah as she moved in our direction. I took a few steps to intercept her and, with a pleading expression, whispered, "Please play along." Then I bent to kiss her cheek. "Hey, babe. Surprise," I said more loudly. "I'm finished early, so I can join you after all." I hoped the word *surprise* would explain the confusion on Hannah's face to anyone watching.

I settled my arm around her waist and met the glare that totally did it for me. A fresh attraction sizzled in my blood. Peering down at her face, angled to meet my gaze, was a perspective I'd never had. I'd never been this close to her, and I'd definitely never felt her warmth pressed against me as I cataloged the freckles along the bridge of her nose and the slope of her cheek. Tonight, I'd have new dreams of her and my favorite bright blue eyes.

Hannah was a few inches shorter than me, and my body blocked her face from the surrounding people. I hoped the girls hadn't caught the moment her shock morphed into suspicion.

I lowered my voice. "I needed to quickly tell those women behind me I wasn't interested. I said you were my girlfriend." Hannah said nothing, raising a single brow. "They're young, likely still students somewhere. Not appropriate, but I didn't want to embarrass them *or* come off as some creepy old professor who assumes all women want to sleep with him."

Hannah relaxed her shoulders as she settled closer. Well, *that* was nice.

"Are they still there?" I asked.

She glanced around me and shook her head. I hesitated before stepping away from her soft body.

Hannah folded her arms across her chest, her very distracting chest, and remained silent. She'd never been one for many words unless she was arguing with me.

"Thank you for not punching me. Can I buy you a drink for being my fake girlfriend?"

Her smile didn't reach her eyes. She was usually all confident swagger, but tonight, she seemed … distant, like that day a few weeks ago in the faculty kitchen.

"Hey, is everything okay?"

"Of course, why?" she replied too brightly.

"You don't … seem like yourself."

"We could argue about why you insist on turning my office into cold storage if that would help," she snapped, her tone thick with sarcasm. Ahh, there was my girl.

"I won that argument already. If you're cold, you can always put on more clothes. If I'm hot, there's only so much I can take off."

A spark flickered almost imperceptibly, and she rolled her lips between her teeth. Huh. That was interesting. And I hadn't imagined it. Maybe …

Seeing her away from campus, away from Bend, I was imagining lots of things now. She wore a dress that looked straight out of the 1950s with a high collar and little black buttons that ran the length of the front. I wanted to undo each one, slowly.

She fidgeted with the sides of her deep blue cardigan—of course she wore a sweater when the bright November day in Las Vegas was a comfortable seventy degrees. The color highlighted her eyes and the red in her hair. I imagined running my fingers through the short strands. It would be impossibly soft, and I could easily move it aside to press a kiss behind the shell of her ear, near those glittering diamond earrings she always wore. Damn it. I needed to change that line of thinking before I "sprang a boner," as I'd recently overheard a student call it.

"Come on. One drink. I bet you could use it."

I saw the wheels spinning in her head, but she only

nodded, and we started toward the small bar above the glittery lobby covered with fake snow, several overly decorated Christmas trees, and a massive train set that wound through the displays. The tinny sound of a familiar carol rang out from a miniature carousel in the center of it all. The holidays in Vegas.

"This place is like being inside a snow globe," she said, glancing around before sitting at a table near the edge of the sparsely crowded space. "Everything is a compact replica of reality and sparkles with fake perfection."

"That's an apt description," I said, not taking my eyes off her face and the single line of freckles that curved along her jaw on one side. I loved that line of freckles, fantasized about it.

"So, what are you doing here, Grant?" Hannah never called me doctor. She also had a master's degree but taught statistics for the sciences and the engineering schools at OPU. Maybe because she didn't have her doctorate either, the assumption rubbed her the wrong way like it did me.

Shit, now I was wondering about ways to rub her the right way.

I cleared my throat and gestured to the hallway filled with therapists and sports medicine professionals. "I'm here for the PT conference. What about you?"

"The race. Formula One. And to connect with a friend," she said.

"Wow, do you have tickets? I heard standing room only along the track was close to ten grand before it sold out."

Hannah blinked again. "No, I plan to watch from the hotel."

"Oh, lucky you. Your room has a view. I'm on the other side."

Hannah squirmed in her seat. Something was definitely off, and again I wanted to help. A drink couldn't hurt. I waved to the bartender.

"What do you like so much about F1?" I asked. "Is it a favorite driver?" I raised my eyebrows suggestively.

Her gaze snapped to mine. "I like the racing, the cars, the engineering involved in designing and building them." Her tone was suddenly curt, maybe more than usual. "Women can be into precision and testing limits, too. It isn't always about the men."

I paused, a little taken aback. There was vulnerability under all that bravado. "Got it," I said as our gazes held and the stillness between us crackled.

5
____

HANNAH

I HATED IT WHEN PEOPLE ASSUMED I LIKED FORMULA ONE only because of the drivers. Racing was about challenges and planning, luck, and engineering perfection. It took a team to win those races, and it was a thing of beauty to watch. That's what drew me … usually.

Grant was right this time, though. I was here, in part, for one particular driver.

My talk with Lorenzo went just as I'd hoped. Once all the other drivers entered the ballroom and the buzz settled, Lorenzo had worked his way to me, casual yet determined, and as the event came to an end, we found a secluded spot for a private conversation. I didn't want this to be any more dramatic than necessary.

I was honest and told him the truth in point-blank terms. He was kind and asked about my plans with trepidation obvious on his features. He said he'd do whatever I wanted, yet it was almost comical how relieved he'd been when I said I wanted to keep the baby but raise it on my own.

Lorenzo and I weren't in love. We were barely friends

and didn't have a romantic future. Plus, we both knew he wasn't ready for any of this, and I was. His shoulders had slumped with his exhale as he bent at the waist. Mister-always-cool had been shaken, understandably. When he rose, he pulled me into a grateful hug, telling me he wasn't sure he ever wanted to be a father, but definitely not now.

We made plans to meet again with our attorneys to begin the paperwork necessary for Lorenzo to discreetly relinquish his parental rights. Neither of us wanted this to get leaked to the press. The baby would be wholly mine.

That thought both thrilled and saddened me.

And now Grant was here, witnessing me in my emotionally raw state. Yes, he infuriated me most days, but he also made me feel things, imagine things I shouldn't. I was pregnant. I just told the father, the only other person who knew besides my doctor, and now this baby was much more real. I was struggling to regain my center. And *he*, with his cheek kisses, intoxicating scent, and soft facial hair brushing my skin, would not help.

I blinked out of the staring contest we were having across the small café table. "So, which one of those girls was hitting on you?" I kept my tone light as Grant used his phone to scan the QR code on the table for the drink menu. There was never a shortage of young beauties parading outside his office at OPU asking for help or … something. I wasn't surprised to see the same phenomenon here.

"Both of them," he said casually. "They wanted a three-way."

I blinked rapidly, processing that development, though I shouldn't have been surprised. Grant was categorically handsome, more so now with the dark beard he grew in the winter months due to all the outdoor activities he seemed to enjoy. Like his hair, it was flecked with silver in places and trimmed short. His eyes were a dark golden brown, not quite hazel, and deep-set under neat eyebrows. And his confident smile was intense and teasing at the same time with one side of his full lips usually quirked up like he had a secret, and maybe it was in his pants.

"A three-way with two nubile ingenues. Isn't that every straight man's fantasy?"

"Not mine," he said, looking up from the menu.

"And why is that?"

"Because I'm not that guy," he said, giving me his flirtatious smile again, reinforcing that he *was* that guy. Hang on to your panties, girls. I was sure my colleague had been melting them since Lorenzo was in diapers. His well-honed skills were unparalleled.

I swallowed and searched for something to say other than *please take me to bed and smile that way while you take off all your clothes and let me lick you.*

Ugh. Freaking pregnancy hormones were relentless.

I collected myself. "What's the saying, 'the boys get older, but the girls stay the same age'?"

"For some, but I don't sleep with women who are my students' age."

"Are you sure about that?" I blurted. Geez, now my rogue thoughts were coming out of my mouth. This was not good.

He blanched. "You don't believe me? Care to elaborate on your theory, Professor Byrne?"

Actually, no. "It's nothing."

"Oh, I think it's something. You and I don't hold back, so let's hear it."

"I saw you once with a young woman. You were having lunch at the international food court and holding hands across the table."

He squinted at me. "When was this?"

"September. Not long after the semester started." I shrugged.

His grin was slow. Panty-melting defcon one. "Long blonde hair she wore in a braid?"

"That's the one," I said, daring him to deny he'd been busted.

His expression sobered, and he leaned close. "I love her. And I won't apologize for it."

I looked away, saying nothing as a surprising sense of loss hit my stomach. The emotion in his eyes sparked a yearning I wasn't quite ready to examine.

"She's my cousin's daughter." He smiled. "I've changed her diapers. Her bio-dad, the dickhead, ran off when she was little. My older brother and I sort of filled the role. David coached her little league softball team, and I took her to the fifth-grade father-daughter dance. I call and we talk. We've always had a bond."

Oh.

"She was looking at OPU's nursing program and came to visit. We had lunch, and she told me about a recent breakup with some asshole who didn't deserve her. She was upset, and I was comforting her."

I swallowed the lump in my throat. "Ah."

He straightened in his chair. "Father-figures can significantly impact a young woman's self-image and expectations of romantic relationships. I told her that douchebag was one of many other douchebags, but decent guys exist who will treat her well, and she doesn't have to settle. We'd been rock climbing nearby, something she is way better at than me. She bested me on every climb, even though I honestly tried." He chuckled, and admiration bloomed across his features.

"So, you don't date younger women," I stated it as a fact.

His gaze zeroed in on mine. "I said I didn't date women who could be my students. I never said anything about younger women in general. Like, for example, how old are you?"

I huffed, but my tummy flipped. "It's impolite to ask a woman her age."

His eyes glittered. "Fine. I'll assume we're close in years, and then I'll say I'm only attracted to women my age."

He stared at my lips and didn't hide it. Was he saying he was attracted to me? The flood gates opened in my mind. Images of him and his firm body pressing me into the wall at that French hotel. Him laying me back on a cloud of bedding and kissing me senseless. Heat flooded my core, and my breathing deepened. I think he noticed because his gaze moved to the pulse at the base of my neck.

Our server arrived, breaking the spell. "I apologize for the delay. What can I bring you?"

Grant gestured to me. "Tonic water with lime," I said.

"You want gin or vodka with that?"

"Neither. No alcohol." I smiled at the woman, likely close to my mom's age and very tan.

"I'll have a beer. Any local lager or pilsner you have on tap," Grant said.

"Too early for alcohol?" he asked after our server retreated.

Maybe it was moodiness. Maybe it was the hope he was attracted to me that needed to be nipped in the bud. Or maybe it was embarrassment from making assumptions about him. Maybe I was just spun up from the gravity of the day. Whatever it was, he'd been right earlier. We'd never held back from each other. "I'm pregnant," I stated.

He froze, then sucked in a big breath as his flirty

expression sobered. "Congratulations. I didn't realize you were with someone."

"I'm not."

He stared at me for a beat.

"Women can have babies on their own, you know."

"Ah. Sperm donor, then."

What? "No, I did it the old-fashioned way, a one-night stand that came with a bonus. Are you shocked?"

"Yeah," he said without hesitation.

I smirked. "Just when you've gotten me thinking you could be a nice guy, all that care for your cousin, you're going to blow it judging me for getting knocked up? I didn't do it alone."

"I'm not judging you." He tilted his head to the side. "I'm judging him for letting you go after only one night." Our gazes locked and that tummy-flipping thing was back, double time.

What was happening? Was this real? Grant and I worked together, sort of. We saw each other a few times a week and only occasionally talked beyond our usual exchange of mostly harmless barbs. We were friends-with-arguing, if that was a thing. Sort of like friends-with-bene-fits, it was hard to suss out where exactly one aspect of our relationship stopped and the other started.

Yes, I thought he was extremely attractive. So did a lot of other women. But we'd never flirted. Never had lunch or dinner or anything remotely romantic. Yet, sitting here with him in broad daylight, I couldn't stop imagining what he looked like without a shirt.

Our server returned with our drinks. I gulped a few sips, my throat dry from my reveal and the annoying buzz settling in my core despite my best efforts to quash it. If he said one more seductive, kind word, I feared I'd jump him from across the table. Pregnancy hormones were real, but this was ridiculous.

"I haven't …" "Does the father …" We both spoke at the same time. Grant gestured to me.

"I haven't told anyone other than the father. It's the main reason I'm here this weekend. I am a racing fan, but he's the friend I came to see."

"He's in Vegas?"

I nodded casually. "He's with Formula One."

"And you already told him?" he asked, furrowing his brow.

"Earlier today. We made plans to meet again on Monday when all the event hype settles."

"Is he a stand-up guy? Is he going to help?"

I huffed low and smiled. "Yes, he is a stand-up guy. And no, he isn't going to help other than signing away his parental rights. I don't need or want his help. I can do this on my own. It was a one-night stand. He's not *the one*."

Grant furrowed his brow deeper this time and chewed his bottom lip. It was actually kind of endearing. He appeared to be debating something, probably whether or not he needed to fight for my honor and if I'd be offended if he did.

"And this guy, the dad, he just agreed to not have anything to do with you or the baby going forward?"

"He said he'd do whatever I wanted. This is what I want, what we both want." I smiled. "Honestly, Grant. We were never *together*, and I don't want to be. We barely know each other. Sleeping with him had been … unexpected. But I do want this baby. I'm keeping it, and I'm going to raise it on my own." I lifted my chin. "I support choice. Some women can't make this choice. I can. I have resources, a supportive family, stability, and health insurance. I'm thirty. *This* is my *choice*."

I touched my palm to my little belly. It wasn't obvious yet, but I was already growing out of anything fitted in my wardrobe. "I'm grateful to have the luxury of choice. Not everyone does."

Grant held my gaze, and it felt like a touch. "You really are an amazing woman, Hannah."

"Because I'm keeping it?" I chuckled.

"No, because you see the world around you instead of seeing it only through the lens of *your* experience."

I smiled because, wow. *That* was a compliment. "Thank you."

He canted forward. "Have dinner with me?"

"As your fake girlfriend?" I teased.

"No. As a beautiful woman I'd like to know better." He glanced at my lips. "We're not in Bend. It's a weekend. Let's take a chance." His gaze held mine.

I cleared my throat. "I'm pregnant, and you want to *get to know me better*?"

His grin was sheepish. "You said this guy's not the one. You're not together, and he says he's walking away, right?"

"Right."

"Then why not? I'm not breaking bro-code, and it's just dinner."

"I'm leaving OPU." The words came out in a rush. "After this semester. I'm moving to San Francisco to be closer to family. Things with the baby will be easier with help, and it will thrill my parents to have me close. It's their first grandchild."

Grant's smile grew. "I'm leaving too. At the end of the semester. My brother is expanding his PT practice north of Seattle. He needs my help to get it started." He rubbed his hand down his face. "Our father passed a while ago, and our mother recently moved into an independent living community there. David carries most of the family responsibility load because he's there. But he has three kids, and he doesn't ask much, so I'm going."

"What about the university?"

"They won't have any trouble finding someone to teach the practicums a few days a week. Any experienced practitioner could do it."

Maybe, but they wouldn't do it as well as Grant. His student reviews were impressive. Almost as impressive as mine.

"So, we're both leaving Bend in a few weeks," I said.

Grant nodded, his gaze still locked on mine as he wetted his lips seductively. Waiting. The sizzle between us roared to a blaze.

I swallowed. "I'm sorry we didn't have this conversation earlier. I feel like we may have missed an opportunity here."

His smile was all white teeth and lush lips. Liquid heat settled in my core, and my pulse spiked. "Or … you could come to dinner with me, and we could make the most of the time we have left."

6

GRANT

This was the best idea I ever had. I was leaving. She was leaving. I was single. She was single. She said she wasn't with the father and didn't want to be. She said it's what they *both* wanted. It was hard to believe any man who had a real chance with Hannah could walk away, but it's what she said. And when the suggestive sparkle hit her eyes, and the blush rose lightly beneath an ocean of freckles, I couldn't resist the temptation. Because it was Hannah. If it was wrong, I didn't care.

I reached across the table and slid my fingertips along the ridge of knuckles where she grasped her tonic water. She wore a gold Claddagh ring on her middle finger. The traditional Irish ring with a heart to stand for love, a crown for loyalty, and two clasped hands for friendship was a classic, and the gold blended flawlessly with her skin.

"This is pretty." I fingered the band. She didn't pull her hand away.

"My parents gave them to my sister and me during a family trip to Ireland when I was in undergrad. Bethany and I both wear it on our middle fingers, so when we flip each other off, it reminds us we're still sisters." She smirked.

I chuckled. "You're close?"

"We are. I'm four years older, so we didn't compete like siblings closer in age."

"My brother is two years older, and sometimes, I think we're still competing."

Her gaze fell to her hand, studying it as she gently lowered it from her glass to rest over mine. She bit her lip and met my eyes. A few beats passed.

I turned my hand to grasp hers and tried to telegraph through the silence how much I wanted her. She seemed vulnerable and so fucking cute. A considerable change from the stunning warrior she was at work, marching into my office, the hard points of her nipples visible in the thin gauge fabric of her sweater.

"Are we considering what I think we're considering?" she asked, her voice low and possibly unsteady. "Because, despite being an adult, sexually empowered woman, and the fact that I am currently pregnant from a one-night stand, I wouldn't call them a habit."

I stroked my thumb over her knuckles. "Whatever happens, Hannah, however many nights we have, this isn't a typical one-night stand ... because it's you. You matter to me, and you have for a helluva lot more nights than one."

She swallowed before a hesitant but definitely seductive curve hit her lips.

I gave her my most inviting smile as my thumb continued to smooth over her silky skin. "About that dinner …"

"SLOWER," Hannah said. "You're putting it in too fast." I

eyed her. Hers were that dark blue fire. Her chest heaved with rapid breaths, and her nipples stood at attention.

Damn key card wouldn't open the fucking door. I was prepared to break it down.

"Give it to me." She stepped in front, snagging the card from my hand. "Let me show you how to do it correctly." She peered over her shoulder in a hooded gaze. My dick was fully hard, and my balls were heavy. This woman was going to kill me, and I'd barely touched her.

Finally, the green light with the high-pitched beep, and the lock released. Hannah turned and I backed her inside, stalking her until her thighs hit the table at the edge of the room. "Are you going to show me how to do other things correctly, Professor Byrne?"

"You're damn right I am." She pulled me to her, and our lips crushed together for the first time. I wrapped her in my arms and shoved my tongue against her lips. She opened on a moan, licking and sucking and nipping as much as I did to her.

"Fuck, Hannah, you taste good." I kissed down her cheek and behind her ear.

She moaned.

"You like that?"

"Yes." Her chest heaved against mine, and she turned her head, giving me more access, thank Christ, before she hissed and shivered.

That was definitely an erogenous zone I wouldn't forget.

She squirmed against me, her center desperately seeking contact and friction. "Do you want to come, Hannah?"

"Yes, a thousand times, yes."

I chuckled. "You want to come a thousand times? Challenge accepted." I pushed my straining dick against her pussy. My jeans and her buttoned-to-the-neck dress were still between us. I pushed again, and she half-sat on the table's edge behind her, then wrapped her legs around me. Damn, she felt good.

I needed to focus. I wasn't twenty anymore. Once I came, it could be a little bit before I was ready to go again. Usually, I could find things to fill the time and keep her interested, but I wasn't sure how long Hannah would let me see her this way, and I wanted to make it last.

"Ahhh …" She made a sound like a plea as I canted forward, placed a hand on the table behind her, and ground against her. "There, yes, keep doing exactly what you're doing."

I did as I was told for several beats, the sound of our co-mingled breaths the only soundtrack. Then she stiffened, her eyes squeezed tight, and her face flushed. Her mouth opened, and she arched but didn't cry out. When her body went lax, a slow grin bloomed. "Holy shit, Professor."

"Are you okay?" I asked, meeting her grin with my own.

"Yes, give me a minute, but yes, I'd say I was okay."

"Room isn't cold?" I teased.

She chuckled. "Damn, that was too fast."

"We have all night," I murmured before pressing my lips to the column of her neck again.

She brought her hand to stroke through my beard. "This is softer than I thought it would be." Her legs still gripped my waist as I hinged over her. "I wonder what it would feel like on my thighs."

Fuck, she was sexy. Hannah was focused, accomplished, and out of my league. To have her here in my arms asking me for what she wanted was more than I'd dared to imagine.

She loosened her legs and let them drop to the floor. My hand not braced against the table, had shifted under her skirt to her ass when I ground against her and it was still there. My thumb drew small circles along the ridge of her hip.

Slowly, I went lower, snagging her lacy panties and pulling them down as I fell to my knees.

"Step out." I lifted one stiletto-clad foot and then the other. I loved stilettos. Correction, I loved women wearing stilettos. She left those on.

"Grant, my legs are shaking."

"Then hold on to the table. It's time for another lesson in doing things correctly." I toyed with the bottom little black button in the long column up the length of her dress. I released it, and then another and another until the fabric parted to the tops of her thighs. I placed a kiss on a group of freckles along the inside of one leg, right above her knee.

"Grant, go faster."

"I thought I needed to go slower to get the green light."

"Oh, fuck," she said. "Green light, the green light is on."

I chuckled and returned to opening the buttons only slightly quicker this time. I kissed the freckles above the crease of her leg, at the bottom of the psoas major. My favorite place on a woman and Hannah's was exquisite. Delicately soft, and when I put my lips there, I smelled her arousal. I wanted a taste. I wanted in.

At her navel, I spread the material wider to see her skin. So many glorious freckles. They were lighter, close to her center where the sun hadn't touched, but they were still there and gorgeous.

I placed a leg over my shoulder and kissed along the inside of her thigh.

"Sorry about … the hair," she said. "I try to keep it tamed, but something about pregnancy and all the blood flow there, it gets out of hand."

I smiled up at her and teased my thumb through the small patch of dark red curls. "You're perfect." With a wink, I pressed the flat of my tongue to her, and she moaned. She was sweet and salty and drenched. I lapped at her center, then up to suck the bead of her clit.

"Oh God. My ears are ringing."

"I think it's your phone," I said, pulling back from my task for a second.

"My what? … What? … Oh … wait." She reached for the device in a hidden pocket of that magical dress. I sat back on my heels, and she pressed the button then raised it to her ear while the other hand settled on my shoulder for balance, holding me in place.

I hadn't planned to leave, though I'd been surprised she accepted the call. That was a bit of an ego hit. Clearly, I needed to concentrate.

"Hud. Something about the rental car. The rental car is blue." She paused. "Right." She focused on me, her eyebrows raised in question. "I think I'll be out all night—" she said, and I nodded, "—but I'll keep my phone and keycard with me." With that, she ended the call.

"Hud is …?"

Her eyes grew wide. Shit, was he the father?

"A family friend. My sister and some of her friends are here too, and I told her I'd meet them. I didn't because I'm here with you, and she was worried. So Hud called."

"What was the bit about the rental car?"

She blinked rapidly, her tell that she wasn't sure what to say.

"Oh, Bethany forgot what color it was." She made a drinking gesture, cupping an imaginary glass and bringing it to her lips as if she were tossing one back. "I know I was babbling, but someone had just had their tongue inside me, doing magical things."

I wasn't sure I believed her, but I let it slide. I had more important things to do with my tongue than talking.

Standing, I let her leg slip down my arm. My dick was barely contained in my jeans. I needed to get us both naked now.

"Oh shit, Hannah. I don't have any condoms. I … haven't needed them in a while. I'll run downstairs and—"

"When was your last physical?" she asked.

"A couple of months. There's been no one since then."

"I tested when I went to the doctor about the pregnancy. I'm good. And … I won't get more pregnant. Do you want to …"

"Fuck, yes," I said on an exhale.

"Then show me what you've got." Her teasing side was back.

Damn, I could fall for her in minutes if I let myself. I wouldn't. Another heartbreak might kill me. But if I did allow it, I had no doubt I'd fall hard for Hannah Byrne.

HANNAH

His eyes darkened at my taunt like they did when I confronted him about taking the last of my favorite pens from the supply closet. I swear, the man invented ways to irritate me.

Watching him strip was no irritation. He'd placed his jacket on the chair-back, toed off his shoes, removed his socks, and loosened his tie. Then, holding my gaze, he whipped the tie through the neck of his shirt with a whispered hiss of fabric.

I finished the buttons on my dress and pulled it off with my cardigan. My panties were somewhere, probably in his pocket, so I stood there in nude stilettos and a royal blue bra. It was the largest I owned, and my little boobs were already spilling out of it.

One thing about this pregnancy, I was excited about having boobs for a while.

Grant stared, and I set my hands on my hips. "I'm waiting." I gestured to the clothes he still wore.

He grinned. "Yes, professor." Too slowly, he unbuttoned and removed his shirt, then pulled his T-shirt over his head with the sweep of an arm.

I loved a man who wore a crisp white T-shirt under his button-ups. There was something so manly about it.

My jaw dropped at the sight of broad shoulders and sculpted arms. His chest was defined but not bulky, and his abs were less washboard than plain visible as he moved. It was much better than I pictured. Without thinking, I covered my slight belly and my waist.

Grant strolled closer, carefree. I wouldn't care either if I looked as good as he did.

"You like what you see?" He tugged my arms away, exposing my body to his roaming gaze again. "Because I definitely like what *I* see." Still holding my forearms, he pulled me to him and kissed me.

This time was more of a sweet exploration, and I sank against his bare chest, absorbing his warmth. An arm encircled my middle, and a hand stroked through my hair between caresses of fingertips along my neck and behind my ear. I loved it. I felt each touch like it was on my clit. I was already back to the climb.

"Pants off, Grant," I demanded against his lips as I undid the metal button and scrambled for the zipper.

"You do it. I'm busy," he said with a challenge in his voice.

I found the tab, hallelujah, and lowered it before uncer- emoniously shoving his jeans over his hips. Breaking our kiss, I bent to push them lower. Grant took advantage of my exposed back hinged before him and unclasped my bra. It slipped off as I curled up to stand. He stepped out of his jeans and shoved his boxer briefs off too.

We stood there, my heels the only stitch either of us wore. I took in his well-cared-for body while his eyes roamed too. He had the perfect amount of chest hair, a soft trail leading to his hardness, and yes, Grant definitely had a secret, and it *was* in his pants.

My mouth watered, and I had to swallow. That was new. Thanks, pregnancy hormones.

He pulled me into his arms.

"Shoes on or off?" I asked, trying to keep the tremble out of my voice.

"Off … this time." He winked and looked around. "You want the wall, the chair, or the bed?"

"Bed," I said and slipped off my shoes.

He pulled me with him to snag the fluffy bedding and pull it down to the foot of the bed. I sat on the cool sheets and scooted toward the center of the mattress.

Grant loomed then crawled closer, settling himself over me, his face barely containing his smile. "I want to kiss every single one of your freckles, starting here." He caressed his lips along the side of my nose, then lower to my cheek as his hand smoothed along my side and up to cup a breast already heavy and achy. He brushed his fingers lightly across the pebbled nub before palming me with a light squeeze.

"Oh, ow," I said. "My boobs are still tender."

"Sorry. I'll be gentle," he whispered against my lips and did as he promised.

He peppered tender kisses on my cheek, neck, and shoulder, blazing a trail, and soon, the fire in my core was back as hot as ever. He was hard against my thigh as he shifted lower, and I wanted him inside.

"Grant, honey, please."

His head rose from my shoulder, his eyes dark. "Say that again."

"Grant, please."

"No, the honey part. No one's ever called me that."

I grinned. "Grant … *honey* … please." I emphasized the word in my plea.

"Hmmm, yeah, I like it." He smoothed a hand along my thigh and up to my center as he gently kissed my lips. "Please what?"

"I think you know." I parted my legs, and his finger easily slid home.

"Ahh, you are so wet and warm. So soft. I'm pretty wound up here, Hannah. If I lose it before you come again, I will make it up to you. I swear it."

He kept that finger moving in and out of my body in a delicious rhythm. I wanted more. "You have me more turned on than I've ever been in my life," I panted. "Please fuck me before I come all over your finger."

Fire blazed across his features. "I like your mouth, Hannah. I like it a lot."

He lifted and aligned himself over me. I moved my legs wider and reached to guide him to my entrance. Up on his elbows, he smoothed his palms along the side of my head, his thumbs at my cheeks. "You're beautiful," he said and bent to kiss me at the same time he flexed his hips and entered me in a slow, pleasing glide.

God, he felt good. Better than anything ever before. Was this Grant with no condom or the hormones? I didn't care.

Gently, he retreated and pushed in again, his lips never leaving mine. My arms wrapped around his waist and pulled him to me. Soon, I felt the first pulse of my walls as the tension built. "I'm close."

He growled, and that alone almost sparked the fire-works. His thrusts grew faster and deeper, and then he rose to his hands, increasing the angle and blissful pressure right where I needed it.

"Oh, yes, … right there, that's it. Don't stop."

He didn't. He only glanced to where our bodies met and then swelled inside me with a curse. "Show me again, Hannah. So fucking beautiful."

The tension broke and I flew. I showed him. And before the shudders eased, he followed.

I woke and snuggled deeper into my favorite heated blanket. I always got cold, and it was wonderful on chilly mornings. The warmth and the weight of it were heavenly. Then I felt the rumble in my stomach rise to my throat. Oh shit.

Pregnant. Right. Here we go to start the day.

With a jerk, I pulled away, partially realizing it wasn't a blanket but the world's hottest man draped over me. I couldn't think about that now. I was going to be sick.

I was used to it. Every morning for the past two months, I'd wake up, vomit, brush my teeth, have a few sips of water or herbal tea, maybe a slice of bread or a cracker, and start the day. I wasn't nauseated any other time, and that was lucky. Some women were sick all day. One little puke in the morning, I could deal with. Plus, it was a good sign the baby was healthy, my body already protecting it.

Crouched above my old friend the toilet, I heaved and coughed. It usually didn't last long.

"Hannah, let me in." Grant said, his voice a little panicked.

"You don't want to see this. I'm fine, I'll be right out. Don't stand at the door and listen, either." I groaned and lost what I hoped would be the last of the meager contents of my stomach.

"Hannah …"

"Grant, I'm fine." He needed a task. "Can you find the room service menu and see what kinds of tea they have?"

"On it," he said, and I heard him release the door handle.

So much for a sexy morning wake-up with Professor Hotness.

After I flushed and pressed a cold washcloth to my face, I opened the vanity drawer and found the standard toiletry pack these types of hotels kept on hand.

With clean teeth and fresh breath, I slipped into one of the terry robes on a table by the towel warmer and finger-combed my hair. A few products sat by the sink and I wanted to sniff each one to determine the source of his manly scent. I barely resisted the urge.

I strolled from the bathroom, and Grant rushed at me with the room service menu open in one hand and his cell phone clutched in the other as if ordering tea for me was akin to calling 911.

"I really am fine." I chuckled. "It happens every morning. It's not like stomach flu. I wake up, puke, and start my day. I am starving, though. What sounds good for breakfast?"

Grant still stood at the ready, not moving. "You're hungry?" he asked.

I laughed. "Yes. I thought we did damage to the room service menu last night, but that was hours ago."

While I was in the bathroom, he'd dressed in his boxers and jeans but left the button open. God, that was sexy. Like one tug of that zipper, and his clothes would evaporate. Good to know the morning sickness hadn't decreased my interest, even after three explosive orgasms last night, or was it four?

He heaved an exhale, and his shoulders relaxed. I lifted

to my toes and kissed his full lips. "Good morning, *honey*." I winked. "Sorry it's early. Baby needs food so I'm awake at her beck and call."

"It's a girl?"

"I don't know." I strolled toward the stylish coffee table and chairs near the window to sit. "I haven't had that ultrasound yet. But biologically, we all start off as girls until hormones take us one way or another. For now, it makes sense to call her a her."

He exhaled another deep breath as he came over to join me. He'd been worried, and my heart gave a thump in my chest. Who knew Grant Robolin was so sweet?

Room service was blessedly quick, probably because it was early. With my belly full of eggs, turkey bacon, and two fluffy crepes stuffed with cherries and sweetened ricotta, I sipped my favorite mint tea. It seemed to be what *she* preferred too because it eased whatever residual nausea remained in the mornings.

"What are you doing for the rest of the day?" Grant eyed me over his third cup of coffee. He'd cleaned his plate of the huge veggie omelet.

"My sister and her friends are hiking in Red Rocks this morning. I love that hike but don't think I'm up for it." My hand drifted absently over my belly. "I was planning to beg off with a headache and hang by the pool or something. I *should* go shopping. I'm running out of clothes to wear. What about you?"

"It's the closing day of the conference."

"Oh." I started to stand. "Am I keeping you? You can—"

"No. I'm not presenting today, and the other sessions

are … not as interesting as you. I'd rather hang out, if that's okay."

"Even if it's shopping and sitting by the pool?"

"If it's with you, I'm in." He winked.

"Wait, are you checking out today?"

"No. I'm here 'till tomorrow."

There was no way I could hide my smile.

8

______

GRANT

Given the chance to spend more time with Hannah and possibly a few of those hours naked, there was no way I wasn't taking it. The closing talks were usually a series of pats on the back to the speakers and a recap of the *great conference*, with most folks hungover from partying their last night away. I wouldn't miss anything.

I'd originally made my room reservations through tonight, hoping to hike near Lake Mead this afternoon with one more day in the warm air before returning to the autumn chill in Oregon. But there were other ways to stay warm and get my heart rate up. If Hannah was letting me touch her soft skin and kiss her lovely freckles, then I would spend the next twenty-four hours doing exactly that.

After breakfast, she dressed and went to her room to shower and change. I tried to coax her into the shower with me, but she resisted. Now, I had a single-minded goal to convince her that a shower with me was exactly what she needed.

I dressed in jeans, a navy-blue T-shirt from the sports medicine group I worked for on the days I didn't teach, and my running shoes. We'd agreed to meet at the bar in the outdoor café near the pool, and as I sat with my glass of ice water, I scanned the area. Several banners splashed with race cars and rugged-looking drivers hung in the bright sunlight.

Lost in Hannah last night, I forgot to ask more about the father. She said he was with Formula One. Was he in a pit crew or something behind the scenes? What were the chances he was one of these guys with serious faces staring back at me?

Whoever he was, it was hard to imagine he didn't want Hannah, and he didn't want his child. I hadn't thought much about fatherhood beyond assuming it would happen someday. I was the fun uncle, the funckle, to my brother's kids, and I imagined a family of my own someday. But now, it occurred to me the years were ticking by fast.

I shook my head, pushing away the rising thoughts, and focused on the sunshine. The palm trees were still, and the crystal blue pool was ringed with white columns and cream lounge chairs.

Hannah and I planned to spend the morning shopping and the afternoon relaxing here. The cabanas at the far edge seemed inviting and possibly private enough for at least a little making out.

"What's the policy on reserving a cabana?" I asked the bartender.

She pointed to a QR code placard. "You can reserve online there." She paused. "You sure I can't bring you anything stronger?" She gestured to my water glass.

"No thanks, I'm meeting someone."

I scanned the code and made a reservation under my room number for a couple of hours that afternoon. It was in the sixties now, but they expected it to get well above seventy later. It was perfect weather for relaxing and sipping something fruity. Non-alcoholic, of course, because she'd sip the drink while I kissed every freckle on her shoulders.

Now that I'd given in to the attraction I'd felt since I first saw her buttoned up and confronting me about the thermostat, making Hannah feel good was all I could think about. I wanted to let my inner nice guy run free for a minute. And doing that with *her* was too tempting to resist.

I'd always attracted women. That wasn't an issue. And women loved the nice guy, for a while, until the exciting bad guy came along. "You're so sweet, such a great person," they said before dumping me for the asshole they *just knew* could be a better man for the right woman, specifically, them. Nice guys finished last. I learned that in high school and kept relearning it through my twenties. So, no more Mr. Nice Guy. I played a role with women now. It was safer, but I hadn't even done that lately.

This thing with Hannah was a blip, a moment. There was no need for role playing.

I scrolled through the lengthy list of hotel amenities and made mental notes about things Hannah might like. A spa treatment. A pool-side massage and snack before a nap and a few more orgasms. Pictures and plans started forming.

We were supposed to meet at ten. It was nearly twenty after, and she hadn't texted. I glanced around and didn't see her. Was she blowing me off? I'd only been the nice guy for one morning. Was I already getting the fucking push?

"You still good?" the bartender asked, her eyebrows reaching almost to the bright blue shag of her hair.

I swallowed, about to order a shot of top-shelf tequila, when Hannah appeared, chewing her lip and looking … uncomfortable.

"Hi," she said and stopped abruptly next to my barstool. "Sorry, I'm late. You ready?"

"Yep," I said, then waved to the bartender as she strolled to the other end of the bar.

I stood and bent my head, bringing my lips close to Hannah's before I paused, giving her a chance to pull away or give me her cheek. The scent of strawberries and something sweet rose between us.

Her lips met mine, and my blood warmed.

"You look nice. I … need this shopping trip more than I realized." She gestured to her outfit with that familiar annoyed expression. Her royal blue bra was visible through the pale-pink fabric of her T-shirt. My dick twitched. Her jeans were snug in places and saggy in others, and she wore colorful flip-flops. The look was unusual for her, miss-always-put-together, but this was Vegas. I wouldn't complain about seeing the bra, but it definitely wasn't Hannah's style.

"No other bra fits, and I don't have a casual shirt that's dark enough to hide it. My belly must have grown overnight because these jeans fit fine a week ago, and now …" She raised her T-shirt to reveal they weren't buttoned. Instead, they were held closed by a hair tie looping through the hole and around the button, leaving the zipper partially open. "I feel like I'm inches from flashing everyone."

I chuckled. "You're beautiful."

She eyed me.

"Even if you aren't as put together as usual, that blush I like is still there under all those freckles." I placed a kiss close to her ear. "Beautiful," I whispered before lightly biting the lobe and pulling her close.

She shivered, and if I wasn't mistaken, her nipples pebbled against my chest. The good professor had a major erogenous zone behind her ears, and I would devote hours to exploring it later.

"Be serious," she said. "This see-my-bra-through-my-shirt thing is so not me. I'm not a twenty-something trying to get laid."

"I don't know. I kinda like it."

She rolled her eyes. "So, you *are* into twenty-somethings trying to get laid."

"No, and you know it. I like thirty-something professors who say smart things through soft, seductive lips. Seeing her bra through her shirt is a bonus." I pecked those lips once again, and she grinned.

HANNAH HAD SEARCHED ONLINE and found a maternity shop she wanted to try in the group of stores inside the Venetian Hotel. Moving from the summer-like feel outdoors to the crush of air-conditioned Christmas inside was jolting.

This place really was like a snow globe with everything scrunched together, even the mall. Greenery and twinkling lights hung from the high ceiling and every storefront, and a live string quartet sat next to an indoor waterway where Italian-style canal boats floated by carrying tourists. The soft notes of Tchaikovsky's *Nutcracker* echoed off the tall white marble walls.

"Can I help?" A small woman with a bright smile glanced at Hannah's clothes. "I'm guessing jeans?" Both women chuckled.

"And either a light bra or a dark shirt," Hannah said.

"Let's start with the jeans. I love this classic Tory Burch style. I think we have something similar." She gestured to the side.

Wordlessly, I watched the two women discuss the selections and fabrics as they strolled past the racks. I noticed a nightgown that would look fucking phenomenal on Hannah. I veered off to check the price.

"Dads always find their way to this section," the saleswoman said as she approached a few minutes later.

Hannah's expression grew alarmed, and she started to speak, but I cut her off. "What can I say?" I told the saleswoman. "I thought Hannah was beautiful before she was pregnant. Now, I find I only want her more." I held Hannah's gaze, a little surprised to realize I'd never said truer words. What would it be like to be with Hannah, have a baby with her?

I pictured a sweet little girl with deep red hair and freckles. Hannah'd be a great mom, determined and vulnerable at the same time. And I'd be the best dad. First, I'd take care of Hannah so all she had to worry about was the baby. Then, as our girl grew, we'd go to the zoo and baseball games, and I'd tell her all the corny dad jokes. She'd grow strong and smart like her mom, and I'd make sure she knew she was beautiful and deserved to be treasured. Anyone, man or woman, who didn't treat her that way wouldn't be worth her time.

Hannah said nothing, and I raised my brows.

"It's an excellent color for you," the saleswoman said, turning to Hannah. "Shall I add it to the dressing room?"

A spark of challenge lit on her face. "Sure, but no peeking, Grant."

"Never." I feigned insult.

Hannah walked toward the dressing rooms, and the saleswoman gestured to a set of maroon tufted chairs nearby.

I took the empty one and exhaled.

"You think they'd make the dad chairs more manly,

amirite?" The man in the other chair looked up from his phone.

"Dad chairs?"

He gestured between us. "These are the dad chairs. All the maternity and baby shops have 'em. I think they should at least make them leather with a built-in beer fridge or something." He chuckled.

"Yeah, I could use a beer right now."

"This is all still new for you, huh?"

I nodded.

"Don't sweat it. You'll figure it out. I was still in the Army for our first. Pregnancy and kids are a lot like being deployed. Long stretches of the same ol' thing between either the most thrilling or the scariest moments of your life. This is our third."

I was silent for a beat, processing his words. "Thank you for your service."

"The Army or having a third?" He huffed.

I replayed my words and grinned. "I meant the Army, but I guess both."

We scrolled through our phones for a few beats.

"Have you gotten the baby books?" he asked.

"I … I'm not sure." I glanced around for Hannah.

He shook his head. "Not for her, for you. Write this down." He gestured to my phone, and dumbly, I opened the Notes app. He rattled off the names of three books. "They aren't that long, and you being prepared can only help. I wasn't lying when I said the moments could be thrilling or scary. Get educated, and you'll be able to tell the difference quicker."

His wife appeared and handed him a small pile of clothes before placing a hand on her back and stretching, jutting her very pregnant belly even more forward.

The man stood and said, "Good luck," with a firm

head nod, and I imagined him as a drill sergeant or something like it.

"Thanks. You too." I watched as they moved to the register.

"You made a friend?"

I swiveled in my seat to see Hannah holding a load of items and giving me a sassy smile. I stood and reached to take the clothes.

"No, I've got it," she said, still holding the question in her eyes.

I glanced at the register. "He was waiting for his wife and told me about the dad chairs."

"Ahh, like the boyfriend chairs at the lingerie stores." Hannah shrugged. She didn't seem bothered that *I* was in the dad chairs.

A curve pulled at my lips. "Um, is that all you need? Or ...."

"This should do it."

The saleswoman swept by and took Hannah's items on her way to the register. I noticed then that she was wearing a different outfit. She still wore the colorful flip-flops, but she wore a bright pink skirt made of stretchy fabric that hugged her curves and a plain white T-shirt. The royal blue bra was nowhere to be seen, and I missed it.

9
____

HANNAH

Grant hadn't blinked when the saleswoman assumed he was the father. My heart did a little flip when he played along. And then he'd said the best thing I could've imagined. The way he stared at that lace nightie, I'd planned to buy it, anyway. But when he said he wanted me more now, I wanted to buy all of them for the promise of many more nights with him. I let the dream linger. Marriage and family and normal.

Though marriage to Grant would be anything but normal. Would we still argue like we did? Maybe, but then we'd make up like we had last night, and God, I wanted more of last night. The idea of asking him to stay the weekend with me popped into my head, but I shoved it aside. It was too tempting.

I stepped to the register, and Grant followed.

"I'll get this," he offered. For a moment, I considered letting him buy me the new wardrobe in retaliation for all the pens he kept from me. I loved the Pilot G-2 in blue, and he knew it. But after those orgasms last night, his slate was clean. Fair was fair.

"Thank you, Grant, but I'll get it."

"At least let me buy the nightgown," he whispered against my cheek, then waggled his brows.

I smiled. I'd been doing that a lot today. "No. It's mine. If you want to see it, you'll have to be nice to me."

His eyes burned molten in a millisecond. "Baby, I'd like nothing more than to be very, very *nice* to every part of you, multiple times."

I swallowed, and the phrase "Oh my" rushed through my mind like I was a maiden, and he was the royal rake about to plunder me in the best ways.

I needed to stop reading Regency romance immediately. Romance plus pregnancy hormones plus Grant smelling so fucking good and wearing blue jeans that appeared to be made for him were obviously a dangerous combination.

"Sounds good to me," I said, attempting an expression of confident boredom and failing. "Hit me with your best nice-guy routine."

He grinned, and I handed the saleswoman my credit card.

"I'll take those," he said and reached for the two shopping bags filled almost to the top. The clothes were quality, not flashy, and I was in a great mood, so everything looked good on me. I threw caution to the wind and bought them all. I wasn't much of a shopper. One of our family's personal assistants had a gift for it, and I usually asked him to do the bulk of it.

This time was different. No one in my world knew I was pregnant. Since I was out with a known companion and had my phone and watch with me, Hud wasn't hanging in the shadows. Also, I'd agreed to check in with a few texts this time and certainly if our plans changed.

Buying the clothes was fun, like living a parallel life or having a secret identity.

"Thank you," I said. "That's very *nice* of you."

He winked and placed his hand on the small of my back as we left the store. God, I loved that.

None of my past boyfriends had ever touched me the way Grant did. The way that made me feel a hundred percent safe, like I was all that mattered. Something in them changed once they learned about my money and especially who my dad was. Money and the Rhodes' last name always changed things, and I never really knew if it was me they wanted or the stuff.

Stepping into the atrium-like center of the shopping area, Grant shifted his hand from my back to thread his fingers with mine as we strolled along the other shops. A delicious scent smacked into me. Savory and deep-fried with a hint of sweetness. My stomach growled, and I froze in my tracks. *Corn dogs.*

Grant spun to face me, our hands still entwined. "Hannah?"

"Do you smell that?"

"The perfume store?" He gestured behind me.

"No, corn dogs."

"Corn dogs?"

"Yes." My head turned without my permission, and I sniffed in all directions, trying to locate the source of the heavenly aroma.

"You like corn dogs?"

"Apparently," I said. Having ascertained the direction of the scent, I started toward it.

"Is this a pregnancy craving?" he asked, chuckling as he caught up to me.

"I don't know. Probably. I've never had one before."

"There," he said, gesturing to a food cart outside the

enormous front doors. We walked through the spacious automatic circular door, moving slower than Christmas until finally, we landed on the walkway and joined the short line.

"Do you want anything on it?" Grant asked, reading the menu board.

"Mustard. Spicy brown mustard if they have it." I was like a woman possessed. I'd never felt this way about any food. Like not having it soon would cause physical pain. And I'd definitely never felt this way about corn dogs.

I hadn't had one in years. The last time I did was at the state fair with Bethany and a few friends while our security team blended in. We'd tried to do those *normal* things like other kids, but Mom and Dad couldn't come. They'd be recognized, and then that could be dangerous.

Once, when Bethany was a baby, we'd been at The Wharf in San Francisco and headed to the Ghirardelli chocolate shop. My parents had dressed inconspicuously and were pushing a stroller like every other vacationing family that day. Some techy bro approached Dad and wouldn't leave, which drew attention. A police officer had to intervene before we were whisked away in a patrol car. I must have been scared because I was told I'd had nightmares for weeks after that day. Hud came on board soon after, and incidents like that never happened again.

Grant and I reached the front of the line. "Two with spicy mustard." He turned to me. "Or do you want more than one?"

"No, I'll start with one." I looked at the vendor. "Pregnant."

He nodded and handed the first prepared corn dog to me like the smart man he was. Grant paid and accepted his own as I bit into the hot, crispy, salty sweetness. I closed my eyes and moaned as I chewed. "Oh my *god*, that's good."

Grant eyed me and chuckled low. "Keep it up, baby. My dick likes your moan."

I squinted intensely at him and snapped another bite of my treat.

"Got it," he said. "No dick talk while eating."

I smiled around the bite.

"Where to now?" he asked. "More shopping?"

"If I said yes, would you hate it?"

"No. I don't mind. You make it fun. You make every-thing fun."

I cocked an eyebrow. "Even arguing about the office temperature?"

His sly grin grew a few millimeters, and if he had a handlebar mustache along with that beard, he would've been twisting an end between his thumb and forefinger.

I shook my head and said nothing. I knew he did that stuff on purpose!

His eyes sparkled, and I bit my lip to keep from saying something stupid like, *I had fun too,* or *I was glad to have a reason to burst into your office.* His fingers hovering above the keyboard of his laptop when I did were damn sexy. I'd imagined those competent fingers on my body too many times.

And then there was the scent of him and the new cedar shelves he'd stacked with books and colorful plastic replicas of hips and knees that separated into parts like a puzzle.

There was always a moment standing before his desk, surrounded by everything *him*, with my hands on my hips, my heart beating fast, and my jaw set firm, that his eyes would blaze and I'd think he was going to leap over the furniture and kiss me.

If I'd known what a great kisser he was, perhaps I would have been the one to do the leaping.

I stretched my back. "Actually, I'm a little tired. I didn't get as much sleep last night as I usually do." I gave him a side eye.

"Then let's head back. I reserved a cabana by the pool for this afternoon." His voice turned low and sultry. "I could rub … whatever needs rubbing—" he smoothed the tip of one sexy finger down my bare arm, "—and you could rest. Massage therapy *is* part of my job after all."

Annnnd, with that, I got wet.

What the hell? The power of this man. Yes, he had sexy fingers, and yes, he offered to rub … things. But getting wet standing out on the street in broad daylight was a first for me.

The Vegas Strip was always an adventure. More so now, with giant glittering Christmas trees on every corner. Flashing lights and ads with almost nudity were the background to all sorts of street actors, including one dressed like that character from *The Hangover* wearing nothing but tighty-whiteys and a BabyBjörn with a scarily lifelike doll inside. There was the seemingly endless billboards-on-wheels flashing ads for *Thunder From Down Under*, and even a shirtless stripper-Santa and his naughty elves, who all appeared to be showgirls working a side hustle.

It was a lot. Adding in the glamour and couture of the F1 crowd only made it weirder. Walkways had been re-routed or elevated in places to pull foot traffic away from the planned race route. Qualifying would begin tonight at midnight, and crowds were beginning to thicken in spots.

Banners hyping the race and teams were everywhere. A rotating image of all the drivers flashed across the side of

Mandalay Bay, twenty stories above us. Grant kept his hand on my back, holding me close and guiding me effortlessly through the throngs of tourists who were pointing and staring up while walking. Men sporting Gucci T-shirts with gold chains and zipping their palms against stacks of cards advertising escorts called out as we passed. Definitely a melting pot of barely controlled chaos. This was Vegas, baby.

Back in the slightly calmer hotel lobby, Grant held my hand and led me to the elevator banks. "Where's your room?"

I blinked. My room. In the big luxury apartment my parents owned at the top of the Encore tower. The one with the black unmarked key card, unlike the hotel's.

"Hannah?"

"Right, sorry. I zoned out for a minute." I reached for my bags, the handles still clutched in Grant's hand. "I'm in another elevator around the corner. I'll meet you at the pool?"

"If I was being *nice*, I'd deliver these to your door." He winked and didn't release them.

"That's true, but I don't want you to expend all your *nice* energy yet. I have plans for those nice hands."

He growled but released the handles as I rose to place a teasing kiss on his lips. I had to keep it light. I didn't want to let on about the whirlwind of thoughts in my head. Like the idea of inviting him to stay the weekend that I couldn't seem to banish.

It was risky. I was the golden goose of catches, and some men would do whatever it took to get me. One of them almost had me fooled, and learning the truth, how he'd lied just to get a piece of the famous Rhodes fortune, had destroyed a lot of my ability to hope and trust.

Money made people mean. Opening that part of my world to others was never something I did lightly.

But this thing with Grant had an end date. He was leaving, and I was leaving. If I let him in on the fact that I was wealthy, not who my dad was, just that I was wealthy, it wouldn't change that. And I was pregnant. My life was about to become so much more than anyone would bargain for, even Grant. It was a fling, not a relationship.

10

GRANT

I was early for our cabana reservation, but Hannah was already at the pool and talking with a group of women at a larger cabana in a separate row from those on the lower level.

"Hannah," I called and waved before slowly stepping inside.

"Grant," she said and reached for me.

I moved beside her, not too close, but enough to place my hand, a little possessively, on the small of her back. She leaned into me, making my hand slide along her waist to settle on the curve of her hip, which was fine by me.

"This is my sister, Bethany." She gestured to a beautiful woman with vibrant red hair, lighter than Hannah's, and not nearly as many freckles. "She and her friends decided to cool off before they head to the hotel's spa."

I nodded. "It's nice to meet you."

"And you," she said with a knowing smile. Hannah must have had to confess to not being in her room last night or something similar because the other three ladies also held the same smile.

Hannah blushed and wrapped an arm around my waist before casually placing her hand on my stomach, right above the band of my board shorts. Even through my T-shirt, I felt the heat and gentleness of her touch.

It took some effort to focus as she briefly introduced me to the others. Emily and Jo were married to Tess's older brothers, and Tess was in a relationship with one of Bethany's close friends. Bethany was hosting the girls' weekend here to celebrate her recent engagement to a middle school teacher in Napa.

Their cabana was more upscale, with a small fridge and sink on one side. It was nice, but I'd rather have Hannah alone, even in the less tricked-out version.

"Our space is right there." I pointed to the cabana I'd reserved. "Would you like something to drink? I'll have it waiting for you when you join me … unless you want to stay with your sister." Please say no. Her sister could have her anytime. The clock was ticking on my time with Hannah, and I wanted every damn minute to myself.

"I'll come with you now," she said, and I threw up my thanks to the universe.

"You sure you don't want a shot?" her sister asked, waving a mini bar-sized bottle of gin. "It's your favorite."

Hannah rolled her lips. "Tempting, but I'll save it for later. Thanks."

I looked at Hannah and kept my face blank as I recalled her words yesterday. No one in her life besides the dad, and now me, knew about her pregnancy. Not even the sister she was currently vacationing with. It didn't mean anything, but something that felt a lot like pride bubbled up anyway.

"It was nice meeting you all," I said. "Enjoy the spa." I stepped away, taking Hannah's hand.

She wore a crocheted type of dress over her swimsuit.

It was cream, and the deep red of her two-piece underneath popped with all the color that was Hannah. Mine were not the only eyes noticing. The caveman inside wanted to puff out my chest.

"Your sister doesn't know?" I asked once we were inside the canvas walls of our cabana.

She shook her head. "I haven't had the chance to tell her yet. I wanted the father to know first. I promised myself I'd give him that."

I brushed a soft kiss across her lips before spreading a pool towel on the chaise for her. "Let me grab that drink," I said and started for the curtained opening.

"I think they come around," she said, peering past my shoulder. "Here we go."

An employee who looked barely twenty-one stepped into the shade at the edge of the space. "Can I bring you something from the bar?"

I turned to Hannah. "Order anything you want. I think they even have corn dogs."

She chuckled and slid her round, dark sunglasses to the top of her head, shifting her hair back and exposing the sparkle of her diamond earrings. I hadn't noticed before, but even in the shade, they glittered. They must have cost a fortune, but they didn't look showy. They looked like Hannah, perfect. "I'll have a frozen lemonade," she said.

The guy nodded and shifted his gaze to me.

"Do you have any non-alcoholic beers?"

"Grant, you can have a beer. It's fine," she interjected.

I leaned down to caress my fingers along the top of her foot. "No, babe. You're not drinking, and neither am I."

"We have a decent no-alcohol lager from one of the local craft breweries," he suggested.

"Great, I'll take that."

I smiled and moved to Hannah. "Finally alone." I

crouched at the bottom of the chaise. "What hurts?" I asked, even though I had a fairly good idea it was her feet and calves. Probably her low back, too.

"Are you seriously going to give me a massage?"

"Yes. And I'm going to make it very, very nice." I winked.

"You know, it would be so much nicer if you took off your shirt," she said with a hooded gaze.

I liked the riled-up side of Hannah, but this coy, suggestive side was doing it for me too. Without hesitation, I stood and whipped off my white T-shirt.

"That is much nicer," she murmured, resting back with her arms above her head and staring at my chest. The action caused her back to arch as she bent one knee like women do. She was a goddess, and I was the mortal ready to serve her every need.

I was usually in charge in the bedroom. It's what most women wanted. But Hannah was different. She wanted as much control as she gave up, back and forth. This was no different. It was sexy as hell.

I reached for the small bottle of massage lotion I'd brought from my room, one of the vendor samples handed out daily at the conference. "How about I start here?" I caressed the top of one foot again, then sat and placed it on my lap. I dotted lotion onto a few spots and closed the lid of the bottle.

"You brought massage lotion?"

"I'm a professional, Hannah."

"You carry it with you like a super suit?" she teased.

"Absolutely. Now lie back and relax."

Our drinks arrived a few minutes later. "On the room, sir?" the server asked.

Hannah made a noise, but I cut her off. "Yes, thank

you," I said, not breaking the rhythm of my thumbs rubbing circles into the ball of her foot.

She took a long drink. "Oh wow, that's good. And the drink isn't bad either." She flashed a flirty grin.

All loose limbs and sultry smiles, she was relaxed and sounded happy. At work, she was refined and contained, deliberate. But something in her expression made me think *this* was the real Hannah, the version of herself she liked best. She inhaled a deep breath and rested her head back again.

I took my time as the quiet minutes passed, sipping my beer between working different muscle groups. After I'd finished each lovely, freckled foot, with its purple-polished toes, I rubbed my hands along the sides of her calves, over the medial and lateral heads of the gastrocnemius, a key muscle for walking and balancing. The joints of pregnant women slowly loosened, preparing the body to carry and deliver the baby. Muscles gradually had to work harder or differently to balance and move, causing those muscles to be unusually sore.

Hannah moaned softly and furrowed her brow though she kept her eyes closed.

"I could do this better if you rolled over," I said.

"You're doing it pretty well as it is."

I stood and offered my hand to help her up, then I lowered the back of the lounger to flat. When I turned, Hannah's eyes had darkened, and she lifted that net dress off, revealing the little red bikini to its full effect. Gorgeous.

"Damn, Hannah," I said and slid my gaze over every curve revealed. Her breasts were testing the integrity of the tempting top, and the truly tiny bottoms framed her beautiful belly. With all her curves on display in that suit, anyone paying attention would know that was a baby bump and a consuming sense of want settled in my chest. I rubbed the spot to ease the ache.

Not breaking eye contact, she sat again and assumed the one-leg-bent position as she rested on her elbows.

"Umm … I need you to turn over," I said, returning to the moment.

"Oh, right. Shit. I was doing so well with the seductress act up to that point, wasn't I?"

I huffed lightly. "Baby, you being a seductress isn't an act."

Her eyes widened. "Wow, you know all the *nice* things to say."

"It's a gift," I said, and for once, it was.

I NEEDED a minute in the pool to cool off after her massage. Touching her skin wasn't like massaging a client at work. I'd had to concentrate to keep my dick from letting everyone know just how much I liked this woman. "I'm gonna do a few laps. You relax. Drink that bottle of water and let all my work sink in."

She was lying on her front with her head to one side. "Yes, sir." She wiggled her ass, drawing my eye right where it wanted to go.

The pool was warm but still cooler than my overheated self. The laps helped to ease the tension in my body. Hannah had me wound up tight, eager for when I could get her naked, and I didn't want to rush this day. It was too good to waste. If I'd learned anything in my forty years, it was that going slow made the finish that much better.

At the cabana, dripping and heaving my breath, I found the curtains open and Hannah sitting in the sun. The loungers were pulled out of the shaded cover.

"You didn't move those, did you?"

"They're on wheels, see. I pushed them. Almost no lifting involved." She gave me a teasing wink.

I raised my brows. "You may have to let people help you as … things progress."

"I know. I will. I have everything under control." She sat back on the lounger. "Come and soak in some warmth. You'll miss it when you get home to the snow."

Sunlight glinted off her hair, highlighting the gold and copper strands mixed in with the deep red. "You need sunscreen," I said, silently volunteering to rub it on her fair skin. I'd be back in the pool again after, but she was worth it.

"Already done. I've been here before, you know." She smiled up at me like we did this all the time, and I realized we did, with our frequent quips and arguments. Except now, it felt like foreplay and the buzz of want in my blood expanded.

I bent down, giving her a kiss, and couldn't resist lightly resting my hand on her belly before sitting on the lounger next to hers. It was possessive, something the dad could do out here for everyone to see, and I was fucking jealous of that asshole. So, I did it and imagined for a second the bump was mine.

I don't think she noticed the touch, or if she did, she didn't react. Instead, she worried her bottom lip, drawing my vision to her lush mouth.

"What is it?"

"Speaking of going home … I was thinking …"

"Yes?" *Please say you want us to get together the second you're back in Bend until the second one of us has to leave.* Two nights with her would never be enough.

She inhaled deeply. "I was thinking, I'm enjoying myself here with you. I was wondering if you'd like to stay the weekend and watch the race with me."

Her expression held uncertainty as if I would *choose* not to stay.

"Fans have all the hotels on the Strip booked. I checked." My grin was sheepish. It disappointed me this morning when I looked online. I'd convince her to see me again once we were back in Bend.

"Stay with me," she said, and her eyes flashed. "I'm here until Monday."

"But what about your sister and her friends?"

She schooled her expression. "They're here for Christmas shopping and the spa, not the race. We're all staying together in my parents' apartment, but we'd have our own room."

My pulse spiked. My next PT clients weren't until Monday afternoon, and classes didn't start again until after Thanksgiving.

I licked my lips. "If you're sure …"

Heat flashed in her crystal blue eyes. "I'm sure."

11

HANNAH

This wasn't a big deal. Yes, it was.

With that one invitation, I'd committed to blowing my cover, at least to Grant. It wasn't merely an exciting idea anymore.

"Then, I'd love to stay." His wide mouth spread with a grin that hit his golden eyes and promised lovely, naughty things, lighting up my lady parts like … well, like the Vegas Strip. "The apartment's in the hotel?"

I nodded. "In the Encore tower. Four guest rooms on the forty-fourth floor."

He considered me. "That's a lot of fours," he said, leaning back on the lounger. "Sounds good."

His lack of reaction was surprising … and perfect. "I'm glad because I'm enjoying *nice* Grant very much."

He turned to me and lowered his voice. "There's a lot more where that came from, and I want to see you in that nightgown, and then out of it, as often as possible."

Once again, wetness pooled low, and I didn't give a shit about the sun anymore. "We have a few hours until qualifying."

He grabbed my hand and pulled it to his lips. "Oh? And what's qualifying?"

I made a face. "Do you follow F1 at all?"

"Men can like things other than driving fast in shiny cars, Hannah."

Ah. He was teasing me, parroting something similar to what I'd said when he assumed I liked F1 for the drivers. Point to Robolin. This time.

"Do you want to go upstairs with me now or not?" I gave him my best frustrated scowl.

He turned overly serious. "Yes, Hannah. I do. Very much."

"Then let's go."

He chuckled and sprang up to gather our things. I slipped on my swim cover-up, and Grant insisted on moving the chairs without my help. That was fine. He could do all the work.

My mind sparked with images of him doing *all the work* in bed. Pregnancy hormones, or Grant and everything about him, made me insatiable.

"Why are the events so late? People at the conference were complaining about noise late Wednesday," he said as we picked our way across the pool deck, now crowded with guests soaking in the afternoon sun.

"Night in the US is morning in Europe, the home of most viewers. Advertising dollars speak louder than our sleep cycles. Usually, European races are on Sunday after-noons, pre-dawn in the US. Late night here, mid-morning there, is an effort at compromise, I suppose. Tonight's event starts at midnight."

I led Grant past the bank of elevators and the large sign announcing the "Best Thanksgiving Dinner On The Strip" to a discreet corridor. I used my key card to open the secure door to the small elevator for the private apartments. Grant noticed but said nothing.

"And what do you like so much about the qualifying event that you're willing to watch in the middle of the night?" he asked as we stepped onto the waiting elevator. He wrapped his arms around my waist, and our reflection blurred in the closed, shiny doors.

"It's when they time each car on the track to determine the grid or starting positions for the race. Until this point, the team, the driver, engineers, and testers have all been working to pull the most from their car. They've tested different aerodynamic parts, walked the route, and tweaked every sensor and input. Qualifying is where they put it all together to see if the team has successfully found a way to get a little more out of the machine than ever before. For some, it's their favorite part of racing."

"Precision in engineering," Grant said.

"And teamwork. Everybody has a vital role. It isn't just the driver. Winning will require the driver and pit crew, and all the analysts and strategists, to be at the top of their game. It's that close."

Grant held my gaze. "I think it's really sexy how smart you are."

I chuckled. "Knowing about F1 doesn't mean I'm smart."

He shrugged one shoulder. "I know. But it's one more thing you know about that I don't. Like statistics. Stats was not my best subject." He smirked. "I've heard students say your class is one of the hardest, but they learn a lot. You're a good teacher." He lowered his voice. "And I've always thought it was sexy."

Slowly, he pressed his lips to mine, and I didn't care about smart or racing strategy or the statistical probability that this bathing suit would fall off my body spontaneously. His lips were gentle but demanding, his tongue thorough in its exploration. Let's face it. The man could kiss, and I wanted more of his mouth anywhere on me.

The bell chimed our arrival, and we stepped into the small lobby. "This way." I gestured to the right and took quick steps as my heart threatened to beat out of my chest.

"Wow, nice place," Grant said as I closed the double doors behind us. He took in the broad rectangular open space with a couple of seating areas, a huge flat screen, and two-story floor-to-ceiling windows above the lights of the Strip. Herringbone wood floors, warm gray rugs, and dark wood built-in shelves helped to warm up the vast space.

"My parents like it. It's warm and sunny here, and it's not far from Palo Alto, where they live, where I grew up."

"I assume your parents are in tech, then? Or well-paid Stanford professors?" Grant asked with a playful gleam.

"Dad's in tech." I smiled, and he wrapped me in his arms again.

This time, his kiss was sweet. Not feverish like last night, or even the sensual tease in the elevator that had me drenched and ready for him in seconds. He didn't have more questions about my dad or this apartment? How we must be unusually wealthy to afford it?

"How about a shower?" he asked.

"You really like shower sex, huh?"

"It's efficient. I need a shower, and I want to have sex. This way, I get both."

I hopped up and wrapped my legs around his waist. A bought of dizziness hit me suddenly, and I slid back to my feet.

"You okay?"

"A little lightheaded. I only had an apple after that corn dog." I checked my watch. It was three fifteen.

"Food's a priority when you're pregnant," he said lifting me against him, encouraging me to wrap my legs around his waist again. "Plus, shower sex requires strength and stamina. Show me to the kitchen."

"There." I pointed to the right, and he started across the space in long strides. "I can walk."

"But I like carrying you. Your body fits perfectly next to mine. Don't you think?" He shifted me so my center rubbed against his length.

Oh, I could probably come from that alone these days. But I needed to eat.

"You're killing me, you know that?" I groaned.

"Right back at you, babe." He stepped around the corner and into the kitchen, then set me down before strolling to the double fridge without a care in the world.

"This is stocked," he said, opening the doors. "What can I make for you?"

I inspected the offerings and spotted leftover mac-and-cheese and cold roast beef. "Let's warm these and have a salad. Good by you?"

"Absolutely."

He prepped the greens and vegetables he found in the crisper while I warmed up the pasta and hunks of lean roast, then plated it all. It was so domestic. Normal and comfortable. And very much atypical for me and a date, or romantic interest, or hookup, or whatever this was. I liked it.

We sat at the small table in the breakfast area to eat and look out another wall of windows at the red rocks of the distant mountains in the sun.

"That was delicious," Grant said with a stretch as he

grabbed my plate along with his and headed to the sink. "Did you make that?"

"Sure, you saw me." I smirked.

He shook his head and reached for the dish soap.

I stood and crossed the room. "Let's put them in the dishwasher. Less wasted water."

"So, Bethany's a chef?" he asked as we scraped the dishes and loaded the machine. "Because that was not run-of-the-mill cooking."

"Jo is a chef, but she didn't make that." I paused. "We have a cook. Everyone's busy doing different things on different schedules. It's easier this way."

He nodded. "Makes sense."

I waited for further inquiries or jokes about what else we had, but he said nothing.

"Do you want anything else? Dessert?" I opened the freezer, knowing Chef would have stashed some individual Ben and Jerry's in there. "Bingo. Chunky Monkey or there are other flavors that will never be as good as Chunky Monkey."

Grant huffed a smile and searched the freezer drawer as I grabbed a couple of spoons. He selected Cherry Garcia. It was a close second.

Leaning against the counter, spoon poised above my favorite ice cream, I was overcome by a yawn.

Grant grinned around the spoonful already in his mouth and shook his head. "Shower sex also requires you to be fully rested, and with the late night planned, a nap first is probably a good idea anyway. I'll get out of your way and let you rest."

"Or you could nap with me." I kept my focus on my ice cream, going for casual and likely failing. "It would, you know, be more efficient that way."

His eyes glittered. "Lead the way."

I TRIED to roll and pull my heated blanket with me. Once again, it was the world's hottest man wrapped around me instead. Smiling to myself, I snuggled against him. I was rarely sick after my naps. Which was good because lately, I'd had to nap in my office a couple of times, and I didn't want to be running through the science building with my hand over my mouth. Sexually active twenty-somethings who took precautions to prevent unwanted pregnancy would suss out a knocked-up professor in a heartbeat.

Grant's cock stirred and swelled where it nestled against my backside. We'd been in swimsuits earlier, which weren't the most comfortable for sleeping. So, Grant had taken his time divesting me of mine, gently kissing the curve of each breast and caressing my thighs. He didn't do more, though the heat in his eyes made wonderful promises. He said he was serious about the nap and intended to relax me.

I called bullshit on that one because he knew his mouth hardly ever relaxed me. He was always winding me up with his words or now, with his kisses. No, his mouth was *not* relaxing.

Behind me, he inhaled against my hair. "You smell fantastic," he said, squeezing me closer to his chest. "And you feel even better." His hand gently cupped a breast and grazed across a nipple, making it instantly hard. Of course.

"Did you sleep?" I asked. Grant had said he didn't nap, but he'd lie next to a naked me for as long as I wanted.

"I did, actually." He glanced at the clock. "Wow, eight-thirty. I probably slept for three hours. You were out for at least four."

I stretched, and his arms loosened, allowing me to roll

to face him, both of us on our sides. I burrowed against his neck and inhaled. "You smell good, too." I hummed against his throat, and he chuckled.

His hand smoothed along my back and side, down to my ass, stroking the skin. I lifted my leg over his, curving around his hip. My core was already sparking, and I wanted to grind against him.

He pulled my center to his hardness, and I sighed. "You like that?" It was an observation as much as a question.

"Yes." So much.

He kissed my forehead as he pulled my center to him again. I arched my hips this time, and liquid warmth settled as arousal filled my veins, the sensation now familiar. I angled my face to meet his lips and ground against him, bringing his thickness to rub against my sex and settle between my folds, already beginning to swell with need.

"Hannah, you feel so good." He guided me against his length once more, and this time, we both moaned. "You're wet, and it's fucking hot. I love how responsive you are."

"It's … new. You or pregnancy, I don't know but, fuck, I want you inside me."

He rolled to his back, pulling me over him and bringing my thighs to straddle the hot, hard part of him. "Like this. You are so damn beautiful, unbelievable, and I want to watch."

I'd never seen myself as anything close to *unbelievably beautiful*. Sure, some men had a fetish about redheads or my freckles, but this was different. I believed him, or at least believed that *he* believed it.

My breathing deepened.

"Help me?" I asked, lifting my hips to find his tip and notch it at my entrance.

With one hand, he held his cock steady, and with the

other on my hip, he guided me down. I sank slowly, not because it hurt or I wasn't ready, but because I wanted to enjoy the initial slide. I needed him deep and hard and fast, but I was teasing myself first, building the fire inside us both.

12

GRANT

She was a fucking vision. The gap below the blackout shades gave the room a smoky half-light from the glow of the Strip at night, but I could still make out her features and details. Hell, I had the freckles on her face memorized and could easily map them in total darkness.

She threatened to kill me with how slowly she took me inside her body, wet and tight. This no-condom thing was intense. I'd had sex without a condom before, back when I was trying to make something last with a woman, but it had never been like this. Damn, she felt good. But then, she was Hannah. Of course, she was spectacular.

Once she was fully seated, she sat back and stilled, her eyes closed, and her head thrown back. Like she was satisfied, but I knew she hadn't come yet.

"Hannah?"

"Wait. Just wait." She breathed, and I took in the vision of her. Pale breasts peaked high. Nipples pink against the brown of her freckles. That bump.

"Feel that?" she said. "Feel how we fit? You make me so hot. I'm drenched and it's all because of you."

I groaned. "Fuck, Hannah. I may come from those words alone."

Her smile was wicked. "You better not, or I'll make you watch my little vibe do the work you couldn't."

Holy shit. There was no losing here.

Slowly, she moved, and I had to concentrate. Usually, I could hold myself back. Make it good for my partner before I even neared the edge. But with Hannah, it was like I lived on the edge, having to mentally map all the muscles in the body to keep from losing it.

I cradled her hips as she rolled down and then up. Each time, it was more intense than the last as she rode me. She lifted her hands and teased the hard peaks of her breasts with the pads of her fingers.

I stifled another groan.

"You like watching me touch myself?" she panted.

All I managed was a grunt. If I told her how goddamn much I liked it, I'd come.

"You feel incredible," she said, drawing out the words between her lush lips, shiny and plump. That fucking mouth. "But I need more."

She rose and slammed down on me. Her "yes" echoed to the high ceiling, and I was lost. Because *this* was Hannah. I was fucking Hannah. I was making Hannah cry out in pleasure, and she was going to come all over my dick.

"Hannah, baby, take what you need."

"I need it harder, Grant. Please."

Fuuuck. Gritting my teeth, I dug my heels into the mattress and gripped her thighs to pull her down with each thrust up. Every time was hard and deep. So deep she took all of me, consumed me as she continued in a constant rhythm. Driving me. Out. Of. My. Mind.

Her walls contracted, a brief whisper of movement,

and I gripped her hips tighter to keep up the grinding pace. Steady and strong.

With a keening cry, she let go, and I couldn't hold on any longer. A rush of wetness then blinding light and heat and Hannah.

She collapsed against my chest, and I wrapped her in my arms, our bodies slick with sweat and each other.

"I think that was the best sex I've ever had." I panted.

She huffed. "You flatter me."

"Hell no, I don't. You are … You're … incredible, Hannah."

"You too," she said. "It's never … It was absolutely the best sex I've ever had."

I held her close in the silence while we both caught our breath.

"I need that shower," she whispered against my neck. "*Honey*."

I grinned at the endearment. "Me too, baby."

We slipped apart, and losing her heat was like a punch, but the view as I followed her into the spacious bathroom made up for it. She turned the handle, and steam rose as she adjusted the temperature, then stepped inside. The slide of her gaze down my body was all the invitation I needed.

Water cascaded over her as she arched into it. Heaviness returned to my dick. I was already getting hard again. There was no way I could have prevented it with all her curves on display.

Grabbing the colorful scrub thing hanging on the shower caddy, I squeezed bath gel onto it and discovered the source of the strawberry scent. Hannah caught me on a deep inhale. "It smells like you."

She rose on her toes and kissed me, her tongue searching, her teeth nipping. Like a flash of light, I was back to being lost in her.

"Let me take care of you," I whispered against her cheek on my way to that magic spot behind her ear. Taking my time, I caressed and washed her, kissing her bump like I had the right as I shifted to wash her legs and feet.

"Grant," she said almost absently. I met her eyes. "You … I knew you'd be like this."

"Like what?"

"Gentle. Kind. Generous. For all our bickering, I knew you were more. Ever since that day you brought me soup. *And* I knew you'd be outstanding at making me come." Her grin grew in seductive confidence as the seconds ticked.

I rose and set the scrubby thing on the shelf before I took her face in my hands. "I've wanted you since the first day I saw you. Pictured you a hundred different ways. Are you saying you thought about me, too?"

She nodded, and something in my chest swelled. Our lips met. I'm not sure who leaned first. It didn't matter. I poured everything I had into that kiss.

"So … shower sex?" she asked.

"You're not sore?"

"I'm sore, but more sex with you? Hell yes."

"I don't want to hurt you," I said. I wasn't huge, but I knew my size could be an issue sometimes.

"Maybe we try a different angle," she said with an arch to her brow.

I laughed and pulled her to me for another consuming kiss. "I like your enthusiasm."

"Yes. How do we do this?"

Wait. "Have you ever had sex in the shower?"

She bit her bottom lip. "No."

Fuck. A first. With me. My mind reeled.

"How about from behind? I mean, not … you know, just …" she said.

"I'm not into anal, either." I grinned. "Do you like it from behind?"

Her expression grew sultry, her eyes hooded. Who was this woman? "I do if you do. I like making you feel good."

"But I like making *you* feel good," I said, pulling her body flush with mine.

"Then touch my clit. You seem to have a way with that part of me."

Pride swelled along with my dick. Damn. A mortal prepared to meet his goddess's every need, I gently spun her around and caressed her hips as she nestled back against me. "Put your hands on the tile there, honey," I said and slid my finger around to that sweet spot at her core.

I WRAPPED HER IN A TOWEL, then grabbed one for myself. She deserved to be taken care of. She blew my mind on so many levels.

In the shower, she'd peered over her shoulder, waiting. There was nothing like smart, sexy, unattainable Hannah Byrne looking at me with all that vulnerability and desire. Only a fool would deny her. I was no fool.

When we were both spent, she'd wrapped me in her sweet embrace and kissed me before tenderly washing me as I'd done to her.

Dressed in plush robes, we sank onto the bed.

"I think I'm hungry again," she said with a mysterious smile that I was coming to associate with this sultry side of Hannah.

In the kitchen, we found a fruit salad and sliced cheese

we made quick work of. I changed into my board shorts and T-shirt, but Hannah stayed snuggled in her robe.

"So, are we watching this qualifying thing from here?" I asked, gesturing toward the large windows in the great room.

"Actually, I have an invitation to a private viewing party overlooking the route."

Oh. I paused. "I should change, then. I'm guessing this —" I gestured to myself "—would be underdressed."

"Not to me." She bit her lip in suggestion. "But I like your jeans and jacket look, too. Very *yummy professor.*"

More clues that the tempting statistics teacher may have had more friendly thoughts about me than she'd let on. I liked it. I loved it. "Which is your favorite?"

"The blue plaid with the almost matching tie," she said immediately. "The pattern is like a puzzle, like they'd go together if you found the right angle."

Hannah was definitely a puzzle, and I wanted to find the right angle.

"That's my favorite, too."

She paused. "Here, take a key." She handed me a black card from a side table drawer. It differed from the one I had for the main hotel. "Meet me here in an hour?"

"You got it." I winked.

13

HANNAH

I HATED WATCHING HIM LEAVE, BUT I HAD TO CATCH MY breath. The sex this afternoon was intense. Different from anything before. Not that there had been many since my first.

A jolt of fear flashed, and I pushed it down. I wasn't there. I was here. I was a woman, not a teenager coming of age under the constant threat of having the intimate details of my life splashed across the internet for comment like I was a panda at the zoo. *How cute. The redheaded daughter of billionaire Mike Rhodes had sex. Will she do it again? Is sex with the heir to billions different from sex with a regular person? The world wants to know.*

Thank God, it never happened to me. But I'd seen it happen to others, most viciously to a high school classmate. I still lived with the possibility of my personal life being exposed to the world for no reason other than people's curiosity, but at least I was past the awkward and fragile stages of my teens. There were some great things about having rich and famous parents, but it wasn't all rainbows and unicorns.

Rifling through my new maternity options, I selected a plain black, sleeveless jumpsuit with gathered fabric at the waist, held with a thick, wrap-style belt that would draw the eye away from my bump. Later, I could wear the belt lower, and the loose cut would accommodate a much bigger bump, making the outfit work for any trimester. Now, *that* was design excellence.

I applied light makeup, styled my short hair in its usual tousled look, and then chose a simple diamond necklace that had been a college graduation gift from my parents. Understated, elegant, and not flashy was always the fashion goal for women like Bethany and me. The less attention, the better.

She'd texted while Grant and I had slept saying she, Emily, Jo, and Tess would be out for the evening, some concert they were attending at the MGM Grand, and would likely be in bed after the qualifying event.

I'd told her that Grant was staying in my room with me for the weekend, to which she gave three thumbs-up emojis, and then I'd texted Hud. He hadn't responded with any emojis, which was actually perfect. In a world without many constants, Hud was a constant, and he cared, though he tried not to show it.

My phone dinged with a text from Grant.

ILuvCold: Hey I'm at the door but don't see a bell.

Me: Because there isn't one. Hang on.

"Hey," I said, opening the door to the yummy professor in the blue-black plaid jacket, dark jeans, and a crisp pale blue shirt under the almost matching blue-black tie. You'd think the two plaids wouldn't work together, but they did. They really did.

"You look beautiful," he said and kissed my cheek. The subtle notes of leather and whiskey in his cologne mixed with clean man smelled divine. "I like those shoes."

I glanced at my strappy sandals that gave me three extra inches. Like a lot of men, he liked high heels. Noted. I might not be able to wear them for much longer and would take advantage while I could.

"Thanks for wearing my favorite," I said, and a suggestive heat flashed in his eyes above his neatly trimmed beard that felt great on my skin.

"So, this party, how do you know the host?" He asked, stepping into the elevator.

"It's not that kind of party. My father has been a supporter for a long time. The invitation was his, but he gave it to me since he and Mom couldn't make it. It's a more private, less crowded venue provided by the teams for VIPs to watch the race."

"Oh, okay. Sounds fancy." He ran his hand through his hair. It was the first sign that he'd noticed my family's wealth may not be the run-of-the-mill tech millionaire kind. "Not my usual crowd, but I'll chance it as long as you stick by me," he said.

"Honestly, it's not my crowd either."

DUE TO THE route through the city streets, we couldn't see the entire track. We had a good view of at least two of the straights, though, where the cars pushed to their max speed before braking only enough to make the corners and maintain control.

There were a set number of laps, and the cars with the lowest times advanced for a second round, then the lowest in that group moved to a third round to determine the pole position and the remaining top positions in the grid. Drivers pushed their cars as much as they dared, and the only competition on the track was themselves and any lack of planning.

Sitting close on a comfortable sofa, we watched the three qualifying rounds mostly undisturbed except for the waitstaff bringing fresh drinks and over-the-top tiny food.

My parents were no longer among the named sponsors for these events, having shifted most of their personal giving under the responsibility of our family's foundation. We didn't have a coveted skybox or a spot on the paddock anymore, which was fine. I was glad to not be surrounded by the chaos below, and since Dad wasn't with me, most people didn't pay us any attention at the party. Hud was there in the shadows, as usual. He hadn't insisted on following Grant and me every time we were out, but he had insisted on being present at this event and had arrived before us at my request.

Grant had been more rapt by the events than I'd expected for someone who didn't watch the sport. I explained the rules and processes and talked about the drivers, being careful not to emphasize any of them, then let him know my dad and I had been big fans of Team Jag for years.

"That was awesome," Grant declared with one last look out the ballroom's wall of windows to the lights along the route below. "Team Jag did well. That Lorenzo guy seems pretty good."

"He has a great starting position for a rookie season. For any season." I kept my tone even.

"So, now what happens?" he asked, sitting forward.

"Engineers and analysts will comb through the data they collected and add final touches to their strategy for the race. Even fans consider past performances, coupled with what they saw tonight, and try to come up with their own race-winning plan. It's like a super geeked-out engineer's version of fantasy football. There's a lot to it." I shook my head. "People say it's just cars driving around in a circle, and I suppose that's true like tennis is just hitting a ball back and forth."

I stood with a stretch and tried to stifle another yawn.

Grant grinned as he rose, then took my hand, pulling me into his body. "Thanks for bringing me. I had fun." He gave me a chaste kiss. "Let's get you to bed." He stroked his thumb along the curve of my jaw.

"Mmm, yes." I pressed a kiss to his lips. "Stay with me? My place?" I whispered against the softness there.

"Okay." His smile was so warm, something inside melted. This one wasn't a threat to my panties. This one was a threat to my heart.

He held my hand the entire walk back to the apartment.

"Everyone is probably asleep," I said, opening one of the heavy double doors and finding the space washed in darkness except for the lights of the Strip glittering through the sheer curtains now pulled across the wall of windows.

Wordlessly, we found our way to my room, and once the door was closed, I loosened the belt on my jumper and heard the whisp of his tie through the collar of his shirt. Like the night before, something about that sound stoked the fire in my core.

His kiss started sweetly but quickly heated as I tasted and nipped his mouth. I rubbed my cheek against the softness of his beard before gently biting an earlobe.

"Hannah," he said, his voice a warning as his hands roamed my back and down to my ass. Deftly, he found the hidden side zipper of my jumpsuit and lowered it. His strong hand parted the loosened fabric and gently caressed across my lace-covered breast. My blood pulsed in my veins.

"Is this new?" He asked against the skin of my neck.

"It is."

"Can I see?"

I stepped back and flipped on the side table lamp. I let the wide gathered straps of the one-piece outfit fall over my shoulders and pushed the rest of the garment to puddle at my feet, exposing my new, golden brown, lacy bra and matching panties that shimmered in the low light.

"I like it," he said, holding my hand as I stepped clear of the fabric on the floor. He knelt and removed my shoes before he stood and toed off his own, followed by his jacket, shirt, jeans, and socks. He was a visual feast of golden skin, hard planes, and smoldering honey eyes that communicated the connection between us.

My heart skipped. This wasn't playful or flirty. This was different.

Still silent, he reached behind me to lower the blankets on the bed, then swooped down to cradle me in his arms, knight-in-shining-armor style, before placing me gently on the cool white sheets.

He followed me, smoothing his firm hands over every contour and curve of me with something like reverence. Intensely, he watched his splayed fingertips glide across my skin as if moving from freckle to freckle along my belly, intending to touch them all.

"Grant," I said with an exhaled breath. My fingers found the warm planes of his shoulders, and I slid them up to sift through the softness of his hair.

He settled himself over me propped on his elbows. With his palms framing my face, he placed caressing kisses on my lips. My heart thumped at the aching loveliness of it all.

No man had ever touched me with such care and

tenderness, and I feared no other man would. He was ruining me for everyone else.

His kisses grew stronger, and I felt his hardness right where I needed him, but not quite.

"Take everything off. I need to feel your skin with nothing between us," I demanded, reaching for my bra strap.

His eyes darkened to a sliver of golden brown around a deep circle of black. With the deft fingers I'd seen poised on his laptop countless times, he slipped the straps of my bra off my arms and released the front clasp with a practiced twist.

Desire surged, and I pushed his boxers down. He removed my panties, and I impatiently reached for him, encouraging him to settle between my legs. "I want you."

"I need to kiss a few more freckles." He grinned and started down my body. His soft beard teased over my breasts with his gentle kisses, making my blood pulse in my veins, before he settled his warm mouth over my center. I was still tender from our afternoon activity, but his tongue was truly gifted. He teased and licked and sucked, slow and gentle, in all the right places until I was dripping and needy.

"Come here." I reached for him, and he slid up my body, stopping every few inches to press a new round of kisses to my skin.

Finally, his tip nudged my entrance.

"Yesss."

Gradually, he inched in, letting me adjust to his size. I was so full but pulled my knees wider to take a little more or him. When he began to rock in a sweet rhythm, I clutched at his back and the pleasure climbed. This wasn't fast or hard. It was warm and soft and easy.

"Don't stop," I rasped.

"Never," he whispered, and my heart thumped. Did he mean it? Could I have this, have him for something like forever? I was pregnant with another man's baby, but in that quiet moment surrounded by him, his gentleness, and his care, my foolish heart wished it was Grant's.

14

———

GRANT

I startled awake in the night and reached for Hannah but found warm sheets instead. Rubbing my hand over my face, my vision cleared, and I saw a sliver of light seeping under the bathroom door.

"No! Oh, God, no, no, no."

My heart jumped, and I was out of bed in a second.

"Hannah!" I shook the handle, and the bathroom door opened. She stood with one hand on her belly and the other covering her mouth, her eyes wide. "I'm bleeding."

"What? Where?" I searched down her naked body but saw nothing.

"The baby, Grant. Something's wrong. I'm bleeding." She visibly struggled to stay calm. Always in control, every action intentional, but not now, and the sight jolted me fully awake.

"How much? What color?" Content from one of the many continuing education classes I took each year for my license scratched at my memory.

"What?" she asked, staring at me.

"How much blood? Was it bright red or something else?"

She blinked at me. "Spots mostly, I think, and not bright, dark like rust. Grant, I can't—"

"Don't go there, Hannah. We'll get you to the hospital and see. Let's not go there until we have a reason."

She nodded. "Bethany. She's across the hall."

"Right. I'll get her. You get dressed."

I threw on my jeans and T-shirt and hustled out to bang on Bethany's door.

She opened and scanned the hallway. "What is it? Where's Hud?"

What? "It's Hannah. She—" Hannah hadn't told Bethany about the pregnancy, and it wasn't my place to tell her. "I'm taking her to the hospital."

Bethany furrowed her brow. "Why? What happened?" She grabbed a silky robe from a nearby chair and strode into our room, searching all around. "Hannah? It's me. What's going on? Did you call Hud?" She asked in rapid fire.

Hud? Who was this guy?

"Yes," I heard Hannah say as Bethany hustled her back into the bathroom and closed the door on me.

"Hannah, I can take you to the hospital or call 911. Tell me what you want," I yelled through the solid wood.

"Not 911," Bethany said with a firmness that surprised me.

At that moment, a man wearing all-black fatigues walked in. "Mr. Robolin. I'm James Hudson. Head of security. I need you to wait outside."

The fuck? "Who? … I'm not leaving Hannah. What the hell is going on?"

"We're fine, Hud," Bethany called from behind the

still-closed bathroom door. "The rental car is blue. Hannah needs to go to the hospital. Please arrange it?"

The rental car is blue?

He began talking into his watch, similar to the one Hannah wore most of the time. All I heard was "chopper capability and non-life-threatening" as he strode out of the room.

I was still back on what the color of the rental car had to do with anything. What the fuck?

The bathroom door opened, and Hannah appeared with Bethany close behind. Her face was ashen, but I didn't see tear tracks, just her beautiful face. "Baby, it's going to be okay. Whatever happens, I'm here."

BETHANY WALKED out from the treatment area accompanied by a nurse. Instinctively, I stood. Waiting. Anxious.

"She's seen the nurse practitioner and had an exam. So far, so good." Bethany sighed. "But I need a minute." She bit her lip, similar to the way her sister did. "Could you go sit with her?"

"Of course," I said like a reflex.

The nurse handed Bethany some paperwork. "Okay, Dad, follow me." I didn't blink or argue about who I was. Tonight, for this, I was the fucking dad.

Hud had ordered a private medical helicopter to transport Hannah to the hospital. "Easier, less interaction with the public," he'd said in explanation. I didn't ask questions; I just climbed in and dared them to tell me I couldn't go with her. I would ask all the questions at some point, but right now, Hannah was all I cared about.

The nurse gestured to a curtained-off area. On the other side, Hannah reached for me, and I recognized the ultrasound machine on a cart next to the bed. I took her hand, kissed it, and bent to kiss her forehead, then her lips.

"I'm sorry, Grant. This was supposed to be a fun, sexy weekend. You didn't sign up for this." Her voice broke, and an embarrassed blush rose on her cheeks.

"Yes, I did. I knew you were pregnant. I knew pregnancy was complicated. I absolutely signed up for this."

A tear welled in her eye, and she blinked, making it drip down the side of her face. I smoothed my thumb across her cheek, wiping the trail away.

"Okay, we'll get started." A technician entered and pulled the curtain to block the doorway. She snagged the rolling chair with her foot and sat. "At fifteen weeks, you're far enough along for a transabdominal ultrasound, but depending on what we find, we may need to do the transvaginal for a clearer picture." Her voice gentled. "If that happens, it doesn't mean something is wrong." Hannah nodded her understanding. "Here we go."

She squeezed the gel onto Hannah's bump and moved the transducer against her skin. The sound of static filled the space for a few beats, and neither of us breathed. Then a fast, rhythmic thwump, thwump, thwump rang out, and the technician stilled the wand.

Hannah made a low, gentle yelp.

"There we are," the technician said with a big smile as she adjusted the monitor for Hannah and me to see the screen. "Heartbeat looks normal, strong. That's a good sign. We'll take some pictures, and then the doctor will be in to talk with you."

"Thank you," Hannah said in a brittle voice I didn't recognize. I tore my attention from the tiny flicker and looked at her. Tears streamed on both sides, and she wiped her forehead with a shaky hand, the one I wasn't holding.

I swallowed the lump in my throat, then kissed her knuckles. "We're going to be okay."

Minutes passed with my lips pressed to her hand and both of our gazes following the clicks and taps on the screen. The technician finished the exam and removed her gloves with a light snap. "That's it. The doctor will be in soon. Would you like some water? Something to settle your stomach?"

Hannah chuckled. "That would be great, thank you."

"I'll be right back," she said and left us.

I stroked my hand over Hannah's hair and gazed at those mesmerizing, countless freckles. Her eyes met mine, and she smiled though her chin wobbled. "I thought—"

"I know what you thought. But that isn't what happened. Bump is still there. Heartbeat strong."

The technician returned with the water and a snack. I opened the bottle, then the wrapper on the granola bar, and handed them to Hannah.

The doctor entered a few minutes later. She introduced herself and leaned against the foot of the bed. "Things look normal. You're fine. The baby's fine. I have no reason to believe otherwise."

Hannah and I both audibly exhaled while she continued, but I struggled to listen for a few beats.

She regarded me and then spoke to Hannah with a blank expression. "While sexual activity is safe for most pregnant women up to the point of the water breaking, when the partner is big … or the sex is vigorous, the cervix can become irritated and bleed."

The doctor glanced at me, and I blinked.

"So, while you're pregnant, explore positions that are low impact. I'll include a few websites and resources in your discharge paperwork. Check in with your regular OB when you get home, but for the next two or three days, refrain from penetrative sex and generally take it easy. Other than that, you can resume your normal activities. Questions?"

We shook our heads, and the doctor left with a brief smile and pleasantries. Hannah looked at me and bit her lip, fighting a grin.

"I'm so sorry, I—"

"Don't," Hannah said. "I was there too. I asked for harder and more. You didn't *do* this."

I ran my hand down my beard and glanced at the floor.

When I looked at Hannah, she seemed on the brink of laughter.

"I don't even know what to say." I grinned a little. "Am I in trouble for having a big dick or fucking you too hard?" Hannah did laugh then. "That was … memorable. Oddly embarrassing and glorifying at the same time."

She giggled. "Typical man."

"GRANT, I can walk on my own," Hannah said as I wrapped my arm around her waist and half-carried her the remaining steps to her bedroom. The sun had just risen, and the sky glowed more purple than inky black as the night faded away outside.

She sat on the bed, her gaze on the floor. The covers were still a jumble from earlier. She went quiet.

"Is something wrong?" I asked.

"I guess our weekend is over."

"What? Why?" I crouched in front of her.

"I can't have sex."

I frowned. "Hannah, sex was a bonus, not a requirement. You asked me to stay, and I said I would. So that's what I'm doing. Unless …"

Her expression softened. "No, I … want you to. We can … go to the race, order room service, argue about something." She rolled her lips between her teeth, and her eyes sparkled, possibly with unshed tears. "I'd like you to stay."

I kissed her hands. "Good. I already changed my flight, and it would be a real pain in the ass to do it again." I winked. "And there are lots of ways to have sex. There's oral and hand jobs and vibrators and—"

Hannah playfully smacked my arm, but I caught her hand and pulled her closer, holding her gaze. Spending time with her was more important than chasing an orgasm. "I want to be here. This is exactly what I signed up for." I grinned. "Now get into bed, or I'll put you there myself."

"Ohh, naked?" she asked with that familiar taunting sass.

"If that's what it takes." I stood and whipped my T-shirt over my head.

15

———

HANNAH

I skipped the private helicopter back to the hotel. Grant didn't ask all the questions I'd seen written on his face during the car ride. He stayed and held me while I slept. I woke about an hour after we slipped beneath the covers for my usual morning puke, then brushed my teeth and crawled back into the warm cocoon he had created.

After my internal exam and initial conversation with the nurse practitioner, Bethany hugged me and congratulated me on the pregnancy. She knew I wanted kids, not that we discussed it often, but sisters knew.

"Is Grant the father?" she'd asked, sitting in the chair she pulled close to the hospital bed to hold my hand.

"No."

Bethany paused, a single eyebrow arched. "Do I know the father?"

"No, I barely do. Remember when I had that awful sinus infection before Dad and I flew to Belgium for the Grand Prix?"

"Yeah, you were worried the flight would explode your head." Bethany huffed.

"I took antibiotics," I said. Bethany paused, and then a light dawned. "I forgot about my birth control pills being less effective because of it. Sex hadn't been a concern for a long time. I didn't think. And then, obviously, I had sex. It wasn't planned. We were both a little drunk, and it just happened."

Bethany said nothing. Her eyes brooked no judgment but held blind support. Always. There weren't many people who understood about growing up the way we did, the privilege, the price, the loneliness of being surrounded by people. We'd learned early to stick together, no matter what. I knew I could count on her to see the good in this if I did.

"I'm not sorry. I wanted to have sex with … him, and it was good. He's not a bad guy. And now I have this promise inside me." My hand drifted to my belly. "I may not get the picket fence of my dreams, but I can have this baby. I want to."

"Maybe the dad is Mr. Picket Fence."

I chuckled softly. "He's young, and I don't have those feelings for him." My heart thumped. Not like the feelings I had for Grant.

Bethany read my mind. "What about Grant? The way he looks at you, I think he'd consider being your picket fence guy … if you asked."

"Grant is …" wonderful. I sighed. "Come on B, it never works with people outside this world. They get caught up in the money, the fame, the thrill of knowing what Mike Rhodes eats for breakfast or something equally ridiculous. Your man is special, a rare find in a sea of entitled douchebags and awkwardly strange geniuses. He knows this world and couldn't care less who our father is. He only sees you. He may be the only man out there capable of it."

Bethany didn't argue. She knew I was right.

"Shit," Grant exclaimed, bolting up in bed beside me, checking his watch.

"What's wrong?" I blinked awake.

"It's almost noon. I never checked out of my room." He shoved off the blankets.

"Let me text Hud," I said, grabbing my phone.

Hud responded immediately.

"He says you're checked out with the card on file, and your bags are outside our door."

Grant paused, his face blank. How did I explain more about Hud and all his mysterious ways without at least hinting at the whole truth about me?

I took a deep breath. It was time to come clean. If he got caught up in it all, we had a natural ending. If not Monday, then in a couple of weeks when the semester ended, and we both moved on to the next thing.

"Why don't you grab your bags and make sure everything is there? I'll grab some snacks and meet you back here to answer all those questions running through your mind."

A curve graced one side of his sensual lips, and he nodded.

Five minutes later, we were propped against the headboard, and I placed a bed tray between us loaded with a random compilation of food.

Steeling myself, I pulled the foil off a blueberry yogurt and sprinkled in some homemade granola. "Alright, what do you want to know?"

"Are you okay?"

I paused, considering. "Um, yeah. Actually, yes. I slept well, and this yogurt is tasty."

He chuckled.

"Next question," I said.

"Are you in any danger?" Again, he surprised me. Didn't he want to talk about how much money I had and who I was if I needed this kind of security?

"No, I'm not in danger. Hud and his team, they're a precaution. When Bethany and I were younger, people made threats against us because of my father's wealth. Every criminal out there figured Dad would cough up ten million dollars and never blink an eye. I grew up with security, but no, I'm not in any specific danger."

Grant held my gaze as he chewed the grape he'd popped in his mouth. "You don't have security in Bend?"

"Not like this. I have my watch." I raised it to show him. "Tracking device, biometric info, easy access to 911, and more. Nobody there knows about this part of my life. I try to live as normally as possible."

Grant chose another grape. "Are you really a statistics professor? You're not a spy?"

I rolled my lips between my teeth and arched a brow. "Those are two different questions. But I'll allow it. Yes, to both."

He frowned, and I grinned. "Yes, I'm really a stats professor. Earned my degree all by my little self. And yes, I'm *not* a spy."

"Ah, whew. For a second there, I thought you were saying you were a spy."

I giggled and shook my head.

"Do you still want to watch the race tonight?" he asked.

"Definitely," I said with a single bob of my head before taking another scoop of yogurt and yummy granola.

"Can I take you to dinner before?" He paused. "A date?"

"Sure, I'd like that." I eyed him. "Don't you want to ask about my family and all of this?" I swirled my empty spoon around to gesture at the room.

"Should I? Is there something I need to know more than your father has a fuck-ton of money, so much that you have to have security to keep some nut-job from taking you to get a piece? You live alone, you drive a red Nissan, and you don't strike me as someone who'd trade on their parents' success or mooch off them. You earn your money and decide what to do with it, which sounds about right."

I said nothing for a beat or two. My chest squeezed, and I had to swallow.

"How do you know I live alone?" I asked, trying to keep it light while my mind raced with the truth that Grant saw me. He didn't know who I was, but he saw the real me.

"We've known each other for over a year, and I pay attention. Mostly, I didn't want some dude meeting me in the parking lot and reminding me with his fist to keep the heat up."

I grinned. "I know you live alone, too."

He raised his eyebrows.

"I didn't want some woman to cut holes in all my sweaters because I kept coming into your office with hard nipples." I pointed at him. "Which I blame you for. It's effing cold in my office."

He sat back. "If you're waiting for me to say I'm sorry, you'll be waiting a while. Best part of my day, your nipples."

"Grant!" I swatted his arm.

"They're pretty damn spectacular. Particularly in that lavender sweater with the white shirt collar and cuffs. It's always a good day when you wear that sweater."

I shook my head. "Yeah, well, your black crewneck is eye-catching. I don't mean my eyes, of course." I smirked.

"I mean those of most females and a few males on campus. You hike up the sleeves and show your forearms. It totally makes nineteenth-century ankle porn understandable."

"What?" He laughed.

"They're all roped muscle and the exact right amount of hair. Makes a girl wonder about the rest of your body and … hair." I bit my lip, attempting to be coy.

"You don't have to wonder anymore, now, do you?" he whispered, his voice like chocolate before he booped my nose with the tip of his finger.

"No, I don't. I have the clear image stored up here for future reference." I tapped the side of my head.

"Professor Byrne, you keep surprising me." He grabbed a dish of kale salad, dug in, and didn't ask anything else about my family.

After our lunch in bed, we showered together. Just showered, and Grant took his time washing every part of me. The man amazed me. He'd seen a thousand bodies. Knowing everything about limbs and muscles was his job. But his expression held a reverence when he looked at me, like mine was special.

I would miss that look and all the touches with skilled, powerful hands. I'd miss his whiskey and leather cologne and his teasing smiles with dancing eyes … for a long time. Possibly forever.

"How about we start our date early?" Grant asked, stroking my hair to get my attention. We'd dressed and were on the sofa near the TV. He'd sat and I'd flopped on my back, draped my legs over the arm like I did when I was a kid and rested my head on his firm thigh. Angled toward the TV, I'd been glued to Sky Sports pre-race coverage for the last two hours while I munched on some trail mix.

"Sure, what did you have in mind?" I sat up and stretched.

"Most of the holiday attractions are up already, I guess because of the race. There's a big lights display called Enchant Christmas at the ballpark. There's a recreated snowy Central Park with a lighted walking path at New York, New York, shopping at LINQ Promenade, and there are tickets to The Immersive Nutcracker tomorrow afternoon. Want to do holiday stuff?"

"The Nutcracker thing, definitely. I heard it's really cool."

He clicked around on his phone for a minute. "Done. What else sounds good?"

"I like Central Park in the snow. I could take a walk."

FALL TEMPERATURES in Las Vegas were excellent. Warm, not hot, in the daytime, which was great for sitting in the sun by the pool. And in the evening, it cooled to light-sweater weather.

For our date, I wore my new stretchy black pants with a tight white tank and borrowed Grant's white button-down shirt, fresh from the hotel cleaners. It draped loose, covering my belly and framing my favorite Hermes cashmere scarf. He wore that wonderful black sweater and pulled the sleeves up to expose his sexy forearms.

After only a short walk, because Grant said I was supposed to be taking it easy, we sat on a nearby outdoor deck at the edge of the Vegas version of Central Park among lit trees and white powdery "snow." Small sofas were covered with domed clear tents that mimicked igloos, and I snuggled close under his arm around my shoulders.

Beneath the canopy of string lights inside, it almost felt like an igloo at the North Pole.

"Are you getting hungry?" Grant asked.

"A little, but this is nice. Let's stay a bit longer." I sipped my tea.

He leaned in and planted a light kiss in my hair.

"You're good at this dating thing. Not that I have tons of experience, but … enough to recognize you know what you're doing," I said.

"Thank you." He grinned, then scrubbed a hand over his beard and looked away. "You didn't date in Bend, not lately."

I eyed him. "Is that a statement or a question? How much do you know about my personal life in Bend?" I teased.

"Not that much. But I hadn't heard you speak of anyone. And no one stopped by to take you to lunch. What's your story?"

I took a deep breath. "As you're aware, a professor dating in a college town isn't easy. The bars are filled with students. If I met someone promising, it would be under the lens of their microscopes. No thanks." Grant nodded his agreement. "My friends tried to set me up a time or two, but things never lasted."

"Why?"

I shrugged. "They wanted to get closer, but I couldn't bring myself to talk about my family, the money. Sensing I was holding back, they'd pull away, then I would, until one of us ghosted the other."

"Why didn't you tell them about it?"

"Money changes things." I paused, debating the wisdom of opening this wound. "There was a guy a few years ago. It took a while, but I thought I loved him. When he met my family at our home, he was awestruck.

Suddenly, he wanted to spend more time with me, make a bigger commitment, lock me down. I was his ticket to the good life. It wasn't *me* he wanted. It was the money. He was changed by it."

I sucked in a deep breath. "I'd heard of that stuff happening with my friends, but I thought I was smarter than that. I wanted to marry him, but I was wrong. After that, I guess I lost faith in the idea."

16

GRANT

"WHAT ABOUT YOU? ASIDE FROM THE STREAM OF undergrads, I haven't seen anyone waiting around outside your door," she noted.

"Yeah …"

She held my gaze, and a beat passed in silence.

I inhaled. "I got a job with the Portland Timbers pro soccer team. I'd had a few jobs right out of school, built my reputation, and this was my big break. I worked hard and mostly ignored the chatter of the players, except for one. He was super cocky, smarmy, had an accent women swooned over, and a complete dog. He treated the trainers like we were his servants."

I shook my head at the memory of the mess and towels he'd leave in his wake for someone else to clean up. "You know the type. Gifted athlete. Good looking. Says all the right things. The world fucking laid down for him, so why not every woman? I … focused on work, not dating, until an accountant in the front office asked me out. We were inseparable for almost two years."

Absently, she placed her hand on my thigh. I stared at it for a beat, absorbing her warmth.

"I took a few days off to visit my family for my mom's birthday. My dad wasn't well, and I wanted to make the trip. While I was there, I decided I was ready to take the big leap. I returned early and was inside the jewelry store ring shopping when I saw them. The dog and my girlfriend were trying to swallow each other outside the doors of some swankass apartment building I'd never be able to afford."

"Damn, that sucks," she said with a groan.

I huffed a laugh. "Yeah, it did. Quit the girl. Quit the job. But not before I'd impressed a few of the right people. I've been consulting on the side with other pro sports teams since then. And now I'm in this beautiful plastic igloo with this beautiful real woman. All things considered, I'm doing well."

I NEVER LIKED to talk about Jessica. The humiliation and loss had landed hard. But this time, it didn't bother me to remember. Thanks to the amazing woman next to me. A woman I would never have had the privilege of giving a few orgasms to if Jessica hadn't done what she did all those years ago. Getting to spend the weekend with Hannah was a rare stroke of luck.

We had dinner at In-N-Out Burger, her choice, after the igloo. We'd gone to the LINQ Promenade to get a jump on holiday shopping and see what sounded good. As soon as she spotted the iconic yellow arrow sign, she immediately announced she needed a cheeseburger animal style. Clearly, Bump had a thing for fast food.

After, we headed to the Wynn for a few hours of rest before the race. The Uber driver dropped us at the roadblock near the paddock entrances. Walking the remaining distance to the hotel would be easier due to the crowds forming.

"Hey, is this safe?" I asked as we worked our way through the crowd forming at what signage indicated was a VIP entrance. "Should you call Hud? Have him meet us somewhere?"

Hannah shook her head and gestured to her wrist. "He's been checking on me. We're good. Sometimes, I think he has drones following me or something equally unsettling, but he's uncompromising in his job." She glanced around the area, and then her eyes lit. "Hey … you," she said, grabbing a man's arm.

"Hannah," the man wrapped her in a hug. He was tall and wore a tailored gray suit. A *Team Jag* baseball hat like the one I'd seen on several others was pulled low.

I met the eyes of the dark-haired woman with him and nodded in greeting.

"I'm Nora," she introduced herself, holding out her hand.

"Oh, pardon my manners," the man said with a bit of a southern drawl. "Hannah, this is my fiancée, Nora. Nora, this is Hannah. Her father … and mine worked together."

"And this is Grant." Hannah gestured to me. "Grant, this is Walker Hewitt. He retired from driving last year."

"Oh, wow. Good to meet you." I shook his hand, then he pulled his fiancée under his arm.

"Engaged? That's wonderful!" Hannah said. "Congratulations."

Walker's grin took over his face. "We just moved into our house outside Austin a couple of months ago. You and your sister should visit when you get the chance."

"I'd like that," Hannah said, and I believed she meant

it. This man was someone to Hannah. Not like a boyfriend, the vibe was more like a brother-type.

Walker gestured to the entrance. "Are you headed in?"

"Oh, no," Hannah said. "We're watching from the hotel."

"Well, come in with us for a bit. Say hello? A few folks have asked about your dad. I know they'd enjoy seeing you."

Hannah looked at me, her eyebrows raised in question.

"I'm game if you are, babe." The endearment was a slip. At least, that's what I told myself. She pressed a quick kiss to my lips, and I grasped her hand. Walker's face flashed with … approval? I hoped so if this guy was important to her.

Together with Walker and Nora, Hannah and I filtered through the throng of people to a gate flanked by four extremely large humans dressed in black with guns holstered to their sides. Walker handed them a laminated card and motioned to Hannah and me.

With our own laminated cards draped securely around our necks on thick lanyards, we strolled through the more controlled chaos inside the gates. A flash of sparkle and hair passed through my vision. Was that Beyoncé and JayZ not more than ten feet away? Next, I spotted the star of the latest Marvel movie.

This other-side-of-the-gate thing was like Oz.

Outside the long building, we stopped near a group of people, all wearing Jaguar logos sewn on their clothes. Hannah greeted a few while I hung back, taking it all in. The hair on my neck prickled. She'd said she was mostly a Team Jag fan. Was the dad part of Team Jag? Was he here now? Something heavy settled in my stomach.

"A lot of famous people are into Formula One," Nora said, trying to be heard above the noise from engines, generators, and the crowd. "Some attend just to be seen. Pop stars and actors taking selfies are one clue." She arched a brow with a head nod at a British actress I recognized making a duck-lips-style pout into her phone. Wow.

"Martin Brundle used to be a driver but now works for Sky Sports. He's famous for his race day interviews along the paddock. He's kinda lovably awkward sometimes." Her eyes twinkled with her smile. "He's a former driver and is a bigger deal to this crowd than the latest DJ making a splash on TikTok. You can always tell who knows about Formula One and who is showing off because those are the ones who don't recognize him. Some even blow him off, if you can believe it." She shook her head.

"Hannah!" A squeal came from the left, and I glanced away from Nora. "I thought you weren't coming."

"Alice Lamaster," Nora said, indicating the woman wrapping Hannah in a hug about twenty feet away. Short and curvy with jet-black hair, Alice draped herself on Hannah. Her strapless dress threatened to flash the goods at any time, though I doubted she'd care. I guessed she'd had a few. The two huddled together for a moment.

"She's a big Lorenzo Messina fan." Nora winked. "I'm sure he's close by. Have you met him?"

"Not yet. Hannah said she knew him."

"Walker trained him, and the team officially snagged him from F2 last year when Walker retired. He's having an incredible rookie year."

"Hey, Nora." Walker waved from a canopy nearby.

"Excuse me," she said, and I nodded before she strolled toward her fiancé and another couple.

Hannah and Alice were still talking closely, and I started in their direction. At that moment, the sea of people beyond them parted, and a guy half-wearing one of those suits with all the sponsor patches approached from the other side of them with laser focus. Alice released Hannah, who glanced at me with something like unease. The man's focus never left her.

My gut churned. I cleared my throat but couldn't look away as the two embraced with a peck on the cheek and his hand sliding closer to her ass than was entirely friendly. And that's when I knew. Young and cocky, parting the crowd like a sports god. Another athlete on the rise with his hands and lips exactly where I *didn't* want them. This guy, this fucking guy, was the dad.

17

———

HANNAH

Grant had been quiet, and I'd worried I'd rudely left him alone too long, having been caught up reconnecting with familiar faces. Priorities changed, and neither my father nor I had attended races as much as usual these last two years.

Seeing Lorenzo was awkward. I knew he and the other drivers would be around, talking with the team, but I'd hoped I wouldn't see him. Not with Grant here. Fortunately, he'd been discreet, our conversation merely a quick hello and a reminder we'd talk more on Monday.

Finally, back in the apartment, Grant and I decided to watch the race from there with the Sky Sports commentators on the flat screen instead of going to the ballroom. And eventually, he reverted to his usual teasing and tempting self, mostly.

Lorenzo didn't win but had a great race. He had a lot to celebrate, possibly with the actress the camera kept spotting in the Team Jag area. After the race, we'd raided the fridge and finished with spoonfuls of Ben & Jerry's ice cream before falling into bed a little after two.

"Good morning," I said to a sleepy Grant as the mid-morning sun glinted through the gap at the bottom of the blackout shades. He was curled around me, but instead of his hand on my breast, as usual, he cradled my bump, his thumb gently stroking my skin. I loved it. And I hated it.

I loved it because it felt right, like the way it should be every day.

I hated it because this was just a weekend.

"Our last full day. What do you want to do?" I asked trying to hide my disappointment.

"We have that Nutcracker thing," he mumbled against my hair. "And we didn't do much Christmas shopping yesterday, what with your burger emergency."

It was an emergency.

"Oh, right. That sounds good. I like spending time with *nice* Grant." I shimmied my backside against the hard part of him that had been very nice, even if it hadn't been gentle.

Grant's lips found the magical spot behind my ear, and the warm buzz ignited in my core. I scissored my legs together to stoke the sensations.

His hand slid from my belly to gently cup my center through my silky panties. I hummed my approval, and he hummed against my neck. As usual, a spark flew straight to my sex.

"How do you feel?" he whispered against my skin.

"Needy." I shifted to roll in his arms.

"Hang on." He held me still.

"You said there are lots of ways to have sex. I seem to recall a few." I tried to wriggle free.

"Morning breath," he said. "Give me a minute." He rolled away and sprang from the bed in his boxer briefs.

"Right. I brushed a bit ago after my wake-up puke."

He huffed. "That shouldn't be endearing, but somehow, it is." He peered around the corner from the bathroom, winked, and disappeared.

Quickly, I stripped out of my tank top and undies, took several sips of water from the glass on the bedside table, and finger-combed my hair into what I hoped was a stylish bedhead instead of actual bedhead.

If this was our last day, I intended to make the most of it. Bring on all the sexy times. They would be my last for a while.

Grant returned from the bathroom looking rumped and completely lickable. I rose to my knees to greet him, holding the sheet at my breasts and flashing my best *coy temptress* expression. I didn't know if I was pulling it off but then flames lit in his eyes.

"Wow. Aren't you a fantasy come to life," he said on an exhale.

"What happens next in the fantasy?" I let one side of the soft fabric fall, exposing a single breast.

He prowled to the foot of the bed, bent to grasp the end of the sheet, and tugged.

I let go and lifted my arms above my head like a supermodel making love to a camera on a sandy beach.

"You are too fucking sexy." He crawled toward me, and I laid back to welcome him. Resting on his hands and knees above me, he kissed his way up my thigh and over my hip. When he reached my belly, he pressed a kiss right in the center then held my gaze with what looked like raw want.

My breath caught and I had to swallow to keep from begging him to do it again. To kiss that bump like it was his and I was too. Like we were two people in love and starting a family. Filled with all the uncertainty and questions but knowing we'd get through it together.

I wanted to beg him for all of that. But instead, I

pulled him to me for a searing kiss. Lips and teeth and tongues were safer than hoping for the picket fence with Grant.

The kiss was intense, filled with lust for his muscular body and regret for the wasted days I spent close to him without knowing him like this. And then there were the wishes. A wish that this wasn't our last day and a wish for someone like him in my life, for me and for the baby. Someday.

When he broke away, it was to hungrily trail his lips along my jaw and his fingertips across my breasts, teasing my nipples. Shivers moved down my spine as the familiar want filled my core. I needed him. I needed him to make me forget how much I wanted him.

He returned his mouth to mine, his hand sliding lower before he gently dipped a finger inside my opening, pulling the wetness there up over my clit, already full and pulsing.

"Grant," I said absently, my body coming alive with his steady, sweet rhythm. He was warm against me, his touch passionate, loving even, and a heaviness settled in my chest.

I needed to move, to force down the yearning inside me and the tears threatening to form. I pushed him to his back and climbed on top, resting my center along his length, still covered by his boxer briefs.

With his hands on my hips, he moved me and rocked himself gently against me. My walls contracted, seeking him, and I absorbed the sensation of him pressing up to me as I ground down. This man who drove me crazy in all the ways. This man who touched me like no one else and saw me like no one else. How would I ever get over him?

I wouldn't. I didn't even know how to try.

His clean, sultry scent surrounded me, urging the heat and vibrations in my core to multiply. He was hot and hard, and our connection never broke with each roll and thrust, each groan and rapid breath.

"Grant don't stop. I'm coming."

"Oh, fuck, me too," he said and jerked against me.

AFTER WE'D SHOWERED, we met Bethany and the others in the kitchen. Her friend Jo, a personal chef back in Washington, had prepared a special Sunday brunch. There were blueberry protein pancakes that tasted as light as the less healthy version, made-to-order omelets, and fresh fruit.

It was a good distraction, getting to know Emily, Jo, and Tess. Surprisingly, they were all from the same small-town Grant was moving to north of Seattle. They swapped tips and stories about the coastal community of Perry Harbor near the Canadian border.

"Did you grow up there?" Tess asked. She had and obviously loved it. Her face lit up when she talked about the rustic resort she owned with her man or her family's tulip farm, complete with a hard-working farm dog.

Grant shook his head. "My parents moved there after I graduated from high school. My brother has a PT practice in Bellingham and has wanted to expand for a while. Our mom recently moved into independent living, so expanding someplace closer to her made sense."

"And you're moving to help with the expansion?" Emily asked.

"Yep, for at least a year. I want to help my brother. Because Bellingham isn't far from Perry Harbor, he's carried most of the responsibility with our folks. I've wandered around a while: Chicago, St. Louis, San Diego. I'm at the point in my career where I can be flexible. I can still consult with professional sports teams and be there for my family."

"Are you consulting with the Seahawks? They have a good team this year." Tess grinned, and Jo gave her a fist bump.

"I'm meeting with their training team in a couple of weeks to see if there are opportunities."

"I mountain bike quite a bit," Emily started.

Jo and Tess huffed and said "a bit" under their breath.

"Anyway," Emily continued with a friendly glare at the others. "Some guys I ride with had to go to Burlington for PT last summer. I'm glad to hear of a place opening closer. I'll spread the word."

"That'd be great," Grant said.

"Working with athletes must be interesting," Tess added.

"They definitely strive for perfection from their bodies, push them to the limits sometimes," Grant said. "It's admirable, the dedication it takes. There aren't many perfect things in this world. Some pro athletes, from a movement and performance perspective, come pretty damn close."

"Sounds like Hannah," Bethany said. "Pursuit of god-like perfection."

"No," I protested. "Not perfection, god-like understanding. That's what statistics are all about."

Grant raised his eyebrows. "I'm gonna need more explanation, Professor."

"Statistics are our best effort to know what God knows, to truly understand the world. All we have are the data points we collect and analyze, and they can be imperfect. Statistics help us use imperfect data to find the truth or at least get close to it.

"My favorite part of teaching is when one of my students *gets it*. Their face lights up when they realize the power statistics can give them to understand and estimate truths in their chosen field, whether it's science or engineering or business."

Five sets of eyes blinked at me.

"See what I mean?" Bethany asked the room. "This is the big sister I grew up with. Disturbingly smart. It was a tough childhood for an average person like me." She glanced at me with a gleam in her eye.

Bethany was anything but average. She was insightful, great with people, and oozed unapologetic confidence like our mother. My so-called smarts were no match for that.

I threw a grape at her, and she caught it in her mouth. "Yes," she hissed and pumped her fist while the rest of us fell into easy laughter.

18

———

GRANT

THE IMMERSIVE NUTCRACKER THING HAD BEEN COOLER than I'd expected. We wandered through the big open room while the story played out in 3D on all four surrounding walls. It felt like you were watching from the inside of the book. And Hannah stayed close or rested against my front, wrapped in my arms. Heaven.

I didn't want to walk away tomorrow. And I didn't want that guy to be *the* dad.

Watching the race with Hannah, I'd tried to ignore the coverage of his car and the camera shots from his helmet. The worst was the commercial for some watch brand I'd never heard of. The guy got out of a Jaguar at some colorful Hollywood-type party, his ironic facial scruff somehow darker than his actual hair. He flashed his watch and a knowing bad-boy grin as he walked away with two half-dressed women hanging off either side of him.

What a tool. Thinking about him made me angry, not at Hannah but at the universe for showing me how it could be with her when I was never meant to have it. Nice guys didn't get the girl. But fuck, I wanted her. I wanted them both.

I wanted to be the dad. It was that simple. I'd already pictured it before I could stop myself. Hannah, round and glowing, then laughing while tickling a tiny bundle with red curls. And I'd be the tough dad rockin' the BabyBjörn and sliding down the big slide she was too scared to do alone the first time.

I was in deep shit, imagining a future with Hannah. She said she didn't want a future with the tool, but he was a flashy sports star, and she was having his baby. No question I was headed for heartbreak, and I wasn't sure what to do about it.

"I liked what you said earlier about statistics," I told her as we strolled through one of the outdoor shopping malls off the Strip. "It fits you."

She squeezed my hand and held it close to her side. "Really?"

"Your drive to understand, to find the truth of something, I respect that."

She smiled. "Thank you. Most people blanch when I say I teach stats. It was clearly a lot of people's worst experience with math. But I loved it. I love it. It's just … cool." She shook her head. "It's hard to describe."

"No, I get it."

"You may be the only one."

Her eyes roamed the window of a nearby gift shop. "Look at all the Formula One kitsch. I should get something for my dad for Christmas." Her face lit up.

I followed her inside and watched as she inspected the gift options, from ornaments and snow globes to signed framed photos of cars and teams. "What do you think of these?" She held a simple rocks glass with a race car etched on the side and a date. She searched the display. "I could get one from each of the four years Team Jag won the Constructors' Championship." She chewed her lip as she examined the selection.

I smiled to myself. It was the perfect gift for a man who could buy anything. Not the glasses, but the reminder of a love he shared with his daughter. "I think he'll love them."

A TV screen to the side caught my eye. It was a clip of Lorenzo, of course. He was being interviewed on what looked like a late-night talk show, sitting in a sleek black chair and dressed casually in clothes that probably cost a fortune. B-reel of him taking selfies with adoring fans and shots of him in a race car scrolled in the background.

"You've had an effect on the fans," the interviewer said, and Lorenzo grinned. The camera shifted to a shot of a studio audience filled with screaming women. Some held signs like "#1 Hot Driver" and "Marry Me Lorenzo!"

"Tell us," the interviewer said, "is there someone special in your life?"

My heart stopped as the camera zoomed in on a blush that had to be practiced. "There is," he said. "But I don't want to say much. It's new and a little complicated." He winked. His posh accent was subtle but there. Fuck, was he talking about Hannah?

She said he didn't want her, and during the race, she said he was rumored to be with the actress the camera had panned to a couple of times. But what man, given the choice between smart, sexy Hannah and some rando British actress, wouldn't choose Hannah? She was everything.

"Yes," she whisper-screamed, pulling me out of my thoughts. She lifted the last glass and slipped it into a box she must have grabbed from under the display table. "This is awesome. If only Bethany and Mom were this easy." She sighed. "Someone on your list who needs some Formula One merch?"

I shook my head to clear it. "I should get something for my nieces and nephew."

"How old?"

"Ella and Janie, the twins, are seven. Christopher is eleven."

"I'm sure they have kids' stuff somewhere," she said, pulling me by the hand. "Oh, how about these?" She held two little backpacks like the ones I'd seen the girls use, except these had the F1 logo stitched in pink. "There needs to be more pink in F1, if you ask me. And you could do one of these logoed baseball caps for Christopher." She checked the tags. "The hat's slightly more than the backpacks, but it'll be our secret. What do you think?"

"How much?" I asked.

"Backpacks are twenty-five. The hat's thirty." She waved a backpack in one hand and a hat in another like she was weighing them.

"I like it. Thanks for the suggestion. I've been distract-ed." I pulled her in for a hug and kissed her cheek. "The kids might not forgive me if I forgot about gifts." They would as soon as we went hiking or biked on the rails-to-trails path along the bay. They were great kids, and I liked to take them out when I visited.

"You're a good guy, Grant. I mean, you're a *nice* guy," she said with her voice lowered an octave in suggestion. "But you're a good guy. You should let people see that side of you."

I winced. "I usually keep my nice guy locked down. But … I've enjoyed letting him out this weekend, being *nice* to you."

I spotted a rack of tiny clothes to the side of the back-pack table. Hannah headed to the counter to buy the glasses, and I added one of the onesies to my pile. I could slip it in her suitcase for her to find later. It may be my only chance to give her a baby gift.

WE DECIDED to watch the sunset over the mountains from the apartment. All the activity was taking a toll on us both. Hannah was tired and wanted to have a quiet night in. I didn't care where we were as long as I was with her. Bethany and her friends arrived home just as the pink and orange colors faded to purple and navy blue.

"Chef is making steak for dinner if you want to join us," Bethany said heading for the kitchen.

Hannah yawned in response, and I chuckled then pulled her in for hug. "Why don't you go rest for a bit. I'll come and get you when dinner is ready."

"That sounds good. Make yourself at home," she said casually as she slipped away, like it was nothing. God, if only my world worked that way.

I rubbed a hand down my beard and followed Bethany in search of a beer. She stood holding four wine glasses and pulling a chilled bottle from the fridge.

"Where's Hannah?" she asked.

"Napping. All those late nights are catching up with us."

"Growing a human takes more effort than we thought, I guess."

"Yeah." I paused. "Hey, sorry for monopolizing your sister this weekend."

Bethany set the wine and glasses on the counter. "Are you really sorry?"

I grinned. "Nah, not really. But I'm sorry you didn't get to spend much time with her."

"Oh, don't worry about it. Race weekends are always like this."

"Hannah hooks up with a guy and blows you off?" I asked with a tease in my voice.

"Yep," Bethany said plainly, and I froze. Her face was a blank stone before it cracked into a smile so much like Hannah's it made my gut drop. "Ha, look at your face. No, you know Hannah. She never hooks up."

"Shit, for a second, you had me doubting."

Bethany's gaze was steady, taking me in. "It was always her and Dad going to the races. Me and Mom shopped or went to museums, and we'd all meet in the middle for a meal or a happy hour. This is the first year Dad hasn't been involved with Formula One much. I'm sure Hannah misses him. It was good you were here."

"Is everything okay? With your dad, I mean."

"Oh, sure. He and Mom are travelling together more. Old folks cruise in Europe or some shit." She grinned.

"I'm sorry I didn't get the chance to meet them. They must be great. They raised two exceptional women."

Bethany's gaze locked on mine. "You love her?"

My heart stuttered, and I cleared my throat. "It wouldn't matter." I shrugged one shoulder. "It's a weekend."

"Ah, using her for her money, then." She raised her eyebrows, but her eyes glittered with her quip.

"I have money. Nothing like your family." I gestured around the room. "But I have all I need, all that money can buy anyway, and I don't need a security detail to live my life."

She paused, studying my face in the suddenly charged air between us. "You know who our dad is." It was a statement, not a question. "You saw our real last name listed on the hospital paperwork the other night in the ER."

I squinted. "Mike Rhodes, right? Hewitt Computers. Cover of *Time* magazine. *Forbes* list of the wealthiest people in the world."

She nodded. "We use our mom's maiden name to help with anonymity."

"Makes sense."

"Trust isn't easy for us, Hannah and me. And not only with relationships, with people overall. But she trusts you." Her focus burned through to my soul. "What if it wasn't just a weekend?"

"I'm too old for what-ifs."

"Indulge me. I'm a billionaire's daughter. I'm used to being indulged." She flitted her hand through the air, but her face was serious.

I ran my hand through my hair. "Well, I guess that would be all my dreams come true then, wouldn't it? I have a great job I love. Living my life with the woman I love and having a family with her, that'd be everything. But I'm not the guy who gets everything or even gets the girl. That's not how my world works."

The words were intense, but shit, this hurt. "She says the dad doesn't want to be with her, and she doesn't want to be with him. But Hannah is perfect. Gorgeous and smart, exciting and challenging. He'll change his mind. He'll want her, and the flashy athletes always get the girl. I don't need to wait around and watch."

"You know who the father is?" Bethany cocked her head in question, and I couldn't tell if she knew herself.

I looked to the side. "I think so. Not because Hannah told me. I saw them. He's famous, every woman's fantasy. He'll want her, and she'll want him, and that's the way it should be. This was just supposed to be a weekend."

19

HANNAH

My stomach roiled. I shifted out from beneath the covers and squinted against the bathroom light as I entered. I was startled to find Grant there, dressed in his usual jeans and a button-up and smelling fantastic, like soap with a hint of sweetness from his beard oil.

"I need to …"

"Right," he said, his gaze roaming my short sleep set before scooping up his things and striding out of the room.

I closed the door with a few seconds to spare before my regular morning event.

As usual, I brushed my teeth and washed my face, then tried to comb my hair into some semblance of a style. Back in the bedroom, Grant stood rummaging in his suitcase. With his hair still damp, he looked better than ever, and he was leaving. Our weekend was over.

"You're packed."

"I need to catch my flight. I have clients at Performance Med this afternoon." His smile seemed sad before he stepped closer. Then the light was there as he drew a single finger down my neck, along my collarbone to the slope of my arm. "So many beautiful freckles. I regret I didn't get to kiss them all."

I grinned. "You got to most of them." I took his hand in mine and met his eyes. "Thank you for staying."

He huffed. "Thank *you* for asking. I had a great time, Hannah."

"Me too," I said, fighting the expanding pit in my gut that had nothing to do with morning sickness.

"Are you with your family for Thanksgiving?" he asked, returning to his bag to zip it closed and pull it from the luggage stand.

"Yeah, I'm flying to San Francisco this evening."

"You're still meeting with the father today?" He looked like he was standing on a cliff edge, holding his breath.

"At noon." I glanced at the clock, then to the early morning rays seeping in under the curtains.

Grant swallowed and studied his hands before he shook his head and met my gaze. "I hope you get everything you want, Hannah. I mean that." The perfect image flashed in my mind of the picket fence and Grant holding a toddler's hand as they strolled around the garden.

"Thank you." I coughed and tried to regroup. No tears.

He inhaled, and the action expanded his broad chest. God, I would miss that. Him. "I should go," he said.

"Grant …" I wrapped my arms around his neck and clutched him close as he sagged into the embrace. This was ending. I knew it had to. We'd see each other on campus for a couple more weeks but that would be it.

Our timing had been off. It was just a weekend, and now I had to protect my heart, or what was left of it. I had the baby and her heart to consider now, too.

He pulled back slowly, brushed my mussed hair aside

with a finger, and bent to softly kiss my forehead, then my cheek, my nose, and finally my lips.

"Happy Thanksgiving, Hannah. I'll see you soon." He smiled and gestured to the black key card he'd set on the dresser.

I nodded, my throat too tight to speak. If I did, I feared I'd beg him to stay with me, love me, love this baby. What we had felt real. But now it was too late. His family needed him in Washington, and I needed to be with my family. We'd missed our chance. I was the girl who could have anything … except this.

He bent for one last sweet kiss and turned for the door.

I'm not sure how long I stood there, my fingers trembling against my lips, trying to hold in the feel of his before I crumpled to the bed in a heap, and cried.

"You're moping," Bethany said from the other side of the sofa. We sat watching some Christmas romcom, our bellies still full of Thanksgiving dinner with my extended family and Jon, my sister's fiancée. I'd told my parents about the baby within an hour of stepping off the plane in San Francisco, and they'd been loving but concerned. Over the past few days, the idea of their first grandchild took root, and their excitement had lightened things more than once.

"I'm sad," I replied despondently. Rather than watching the movie, I kept replaying my weekend with Grant and picturing him with a little bundle in that onesie he'd slipped in my suitcase with a simple note of congratulations that had brought fresh tears. God, I missed him.

The conversation with the lawyers and signing the necessary documents with Lorenzo had gone well.

"I'm not sorry," I'd told him, "and I don't want you to be. This was a gift. I've wanted a family but never believed

I could have it with everything else in my life." He nodded his understanding. Lorenzo knew this world as well as I did. "Now I can. This baby will have love and a family. I'll make sure of it."

He'd pulled me into an embrace, and I almost felt maternal. After all, he was young, practically still a boy who'd been away from home for years, playing in a man's world.

Everything would be finalized in the coming weeks, and the lawyers would exchange copies of all we'd signed. For medical reasons, I would list Lorenzo on the birth certificate in case of future genetic issues or other concerns, but otherwise, he was not the baby's father.

As I said goodbye to him, a picture of Grant, his focus locked on the ultrasound monitor, flashed in my mind. He'd been utterly captivated by the little flashing heartbeat. My baby needed a dad like that.

"What will it take for you to be unsad?" Bethany asked, nudging her foot against my leg.

"I don't know."

"Sure you do," she said like it was simple.

"What?" I frowned at her.

"The father." She gestured to my belly.

"What about him?"

"It's Lorenzo, isn't it? I saw you looking too long at that photo of him in Dad's office. The one with Mr. Hewitt and Walker."

"No," I said with an emphatic raise of my chin.

"No?" her eyebrows hit her hairline.

"Not anymore. He signed away his parental rights. I asked him to, and he agreed. The baby is mine. Well, as soon as the judge signs off."

She didn't miss a beat. "Grant would make a good

father." She said it like she was saying he would make good chocolate chip cookies.

"Bethany, don't start."

"Why? You said you didn't want to talk about him because it was Thanksgiving. Well, Thanksgiving is done. It's time to talk about him."

"What do you want me to say?" I sighed and shifted to shake my leg, which had fallen asleep in my dazed state.

"Why'd you want Lorenzo to give up his rights?"

I blinked at the subject change. "He would be a disaster. I wouldn't do that to him or me or the baby. The only good thing about Lorenzo and I trying to make a go of it would be that I'd know he wasn't with me because of Dad."

"You're right. It'd be about the baby. But if you were with Grant, it would be about you. And the baby, I think, but mostly you."

I shook my head, mentally stacking bricks between my heart and the idea. "Grant wouldn't know what he was getting into. If I truly peeled back the veil and he turned out to be like the others, it would crush me. No. This isn't just about me anymore. It's about the baby, too. How can I be sure that he wouldn't see the stuff and the fame, and we'd get lost along the way like with everyone else before him?"

"I don't think the fame and money matter to him."

"You don't think it would matter when he found out our dad is Mike Rhodes, the goddamn Founders' Myth come to life? The media always presents Dad as a caricature of a tech genius *ordained* for this success rather than a human who loves to tinker and got lucky. The possibility that Dad's greatness might rub off is intoxicating to some. It's mattered to all the others I let into this world."

"Grant knows about Dad."

I frowned at her. "What?"

"We talked about it on Sunday, while you were sleeping."

Wait. I sat up. "You told him?" My voice rose in anger or fear or something.

"No, he knew since the hospital. He saw your legal name on the paperwork, and everyone quietly shuffling you into a restricted area with limited staff like you were the president didn't help. It wasn't a big leap."

He'd known since the hospital? "But … he didn't act any differently after that. Are you sure?" I asked.

She pursed her lips, waiting for me to say more. But I was at a loss for words. Grant had known for days? He'd known when he said I was the type to stand on my own, when he teased me, and when he touched me so tenderly I almost cried.

"He said *nothing*, and then he left without some sort of desperate plea for more." I was stunned. No one else had done that.

"Yep, because it's what you asked for, a weekend. He fucking loves you. *You*, Hannah. Like Jon loves me. Grant hasn't read about Dad in *People* magazine and thought, 'I could tolerate his daughter if she came with all that stuff' like you're some oil princess. He doesn't give a shit about Dad. He just wants you. It was written all over his face on Sunday. He loves you and walked away because you didn't ask him to stay. I think he'd do anything for you, even break his own heart, because that's exactly what it looked like."

Grant knew. And he still saw me, the real me. "Bethany … Could I have this?"

"Yep, but you gotta go get it. And don't think I don't

know how scared you are. But you told me to suck it up after I broke my heart pining for a man who loved someone else. Now, I'm saying it to you. If you want your dream, get off your ass and go get it."

20

GRANT

It was for the best. I wasn't the guy who got to rescue the damsel and ride off into the sunset. But damn, this time, I wanted it so bad my chest hurt.

For a few brief hours on Monday and Tuesday, I'd put her out of my mind and concentrated on my clients at the orthopedic medical center. Otherwise, I relived every minute. The light in her eyes, her sharp wit, and the softness of her skin with each tempting freckle. Despite my desperate attempt to keep my heart locked down, I'd fallen for Hannah, probably long before the weekend.

I loved her. Really loved her, like no one before.

Bethany said it was hard for them to trust, and it made me want to hold Hannah closer, earn her trust until she knew in her bones how completely amazing she was. But that wasn't my job. That job belonged to someone else. I tried not to think about him.

I made it to David's house in Bellingham late Wednesday after I'd flown to Seattle to meet with the training staff for the Seahawks football team. The Hawks had a beautiful facility on the southeast side of Lake Washington, and by the end of the meeting, we had a plan in place for me to work with a few of their starters who were still nursing injuries from earlier in the season.

I spent the holiday gathering with my family at a table heavy with turkey, cranberry sauce, roasted green beans, and Mom's classic pumpkin stuffed ravioli with brown butter and sage, a traditional nod to our Italian heritage.

Dinner was at David's house for the first time instead of the large Victorian home Mom and Dad had retired to years ago.

They'd wanted to be near the water and have enough space for long visits from the grandkids. When David and his family settled in nearby Bellingham, I'd been the only one visiting from far away. With no wife and kids in tow to fill the rooms, the emptiness of unmet expectations had grown loud in my ears every time I set foot in that house. It was a mercy to not be there this year.

There was another upside to the location change. David's media room, a.k.a. the basement, with a gas fireplace, stocked beer fridge, and huge TV to watch sports, was a classic man cave. Perfect for nursing a broken heart with manly grunts and shouts at the referees.

"It won't hurt business to advertise your consulting with pro athletes," David said as the Seahawks took a timeout. "With the yacht and second-home crowd, Perry Harbor has a few more rich elites per capita than Bellingham. They'll eat that up."

At least I had a great career.

Friday was traditionally my day with the kids, and they requested a ride on the long rails-to-trails path in Perry

Harbor. The town would soon be my home, so I obliged, and though it had misted rain during the few hours of daylight, we'd managed a bike ride around the bay and hot chocolate at the food trucks parked by the marina.

Strings of twinkle lights glowed from every tree in town. Not quite the lights of Vegas, but it still made me think of Hannah. Would Lorenzo-the-flashy-driver take her and the girl on bike rides through trees laced with colorful lights?

The hot chocolate had worn off, and the girls talked me into trying the "super special holiday surprise cookie" from Shakey Grounds Café on our way back to the truck. Watching the kids walk their bikes up the sidewalk, I nearly collided with Bethany's friend Emily as she strolled out of the local coffee shop and lunch spot. The smell of sugar and cinnamon trailed after her.

"Grant! Hi! I didn't know you were moving so soon," she said with a warm smile and questioning glance at the kids. A big guy in mountain biking shorts and a jersey stepped behind her. "Finn, this is Grant. He's with Hannah, Bethany's sister. We met last weekend. Grant, this is my husband, Finn."

Finn reached out. "Good to meet you."

"This is my nephew Christopher, and these are my nieces, Ella and Janie." I gestured to each one.

"That's a cool bike," Christopher said to Finn eyeing his e-mountain bike as he pulled it from the rack beside us. Christopher started in with questions, and the girls scooted closer.

"Hey Chris, back off, dude," I said with a chuckle.

"Oh, let him ask. Finn loves to talk bikes." Emily's expression was thoughtful as she watched her husband patiently point out the electric components and gears.

"I still have a few weeks before I move," I said. "I'm

here with my family for the holiday. Then, in a couple of weeks, I'll look for a house and figure out the timing."

"Is Hannah coming with you? Bethany mentioned she wanted to live in a small town after the baby's born."

I felt a punch and must have winced because Emily's expression grew alarmed. "I'm sorry, did you guys … break up?"

"No, no, we were never together. We're friends. The weekend was … special. It probably wouldn't have happened if we weren't going our separate ways in a couple of weeks."

"Oh, I'm sorry. I thought you guys were a couple. You … seemed so happy."

"It's okay. It was fun. No a big deal."

Emily's expression said she didn't buy my story.

I swiveled to the kids. "Come on guys, let's get those cookies so you can ride 'em off before this mist turns to real rain."

We said our goodbyes and Emily and Finn walked their bikes down the sidewalk to the street. I'd see them again, and each time would be a reminder of Hannah. Fuck my life.

"What's wrong?" Mom asked while I helped her roll gnocchi in David's kitchen on Friday evening.

"Nothing."

"Don't give me nothing, mister." She pinned me with a look that said absolutely no bullshit tolerated.

"A friend. With the move, I won't see her anymore."

"A friend?" Mom said. Her tone rose in question, though she kept her eyes focused on flouring the dough she was kneading.

"Yeah." I concentrated on my fork, cutting and pressing the fluffy potato pillows in the traditional way Mom had shown David and me when we still needed to stand on kitchen chairs to reach the counter. The fantasy of watching my mom next to a little girl with loose red curls standing on a chair and rolling gnocchi with sticky fingers didn't help my mood.

I had to stop doing this to myself.

Memories of Hannah's laugh or frustrated glare had entered my mind on repeat, coupled with images of her in the half-light of the dark bedroom and the sparkling city lights beyond the glass.

My heart ached. I wanted *everything*. My job, consulting with athletes, coming home to Hannah and the baby, and riding bikes in this homey small town. Goddamnit.

"GRANT, can we touch base on a couple of business items after your next client?" David asked from the office doorway as I headed to the waiting area. It was Saturday, and I was helping in the Bellingham office to get a feel for how things ran. It had been busy with the practice closed on Thursday and Friday.

"Sounds good," I said and checked the name of the next client. My steps stuttered.

Reid Hastings was a super-jock and all-state football star from my days as an athletic trainer for our high school team. Across the waiting room, he stood with effort in worn Carhartt pants and a dark green, long-sleeved T-shirt.

I took a deep breath and kept my tone professional. "Reid. Hi, we're a little full, so I'll be working with you today."

He walked over with an obvious hitch in his gate.

"Grant," I said, introducing myself.

"Hey man, I remember. It's been a long time." His smile was genuine. I wasn't sure I'd seen that version of the smile that made girls, teachers, and football fans fall at his feet.

Reid had been my high school's golden boy. He didn't study, but teachers passed him anyway because he needed the grades to play football. He dated the nicest girls and treated them like crap. Yet they kept going back for more. All of them. Good guys never stood a chance.

After high school, he'd gotten a full ride to Udub with grades he hadn't earned. I had a work-study program and student loans that took years to pay off. When he went sixth in the NFL draft five years later, I decided that if I was ever able to work with professional sports teams, I'd stick to soccer and baseball.

Several years ago, I stopped keeping that promise. The fact that the timing coincided with news Reid blew out his knee on a career-ending tackle was unrelated. Mostly.

"Right." I reached out to shake his hand and led him back to the open gym and treatment area. "I didn't realize you lived here."

"I finished my degree at Western a few years ago. It made sense to move, and the family didn't mind."

"What's your degree?"

"Education. Actually, I just got my masters in the spring. Turns out, I'm not a stupid jock after all."

Huh. Okay.

"I think you're on a good track with this treatment plan," I said, bringing the conversation to more familiar territory. "You're still having balance issues?"

He nodded. "Is there anything you would change?"

I pulled up his X-rays and history on the laptop. "Maybe a couple of things. There've been a few recent advances in what we know about how muscles compensate for weaker ones. I can make a note for Tasha. She's a solid therapist. You're in excellent hands."

Reid nodded. "You've worked with a lot of pros. I appreciate your input."

"You know someone I've treated?" I asked, motioning him to the treadmill for a light warm-up.

"A few, but you have a reputation with the players. Pro sports is not a big world."

I scratched my fingers through my beard, stunned that he'd heard of my work, and his expression held something like respect.

"Everyone says you're the best. Everyone I've talked to, at least. I wasn't surprised. You were the best trainer we had in high school, and you had your shit together. I wish I'd been more like that, if I'm being honest."

I must have gaped, but shock had frozen my speech.

He laughed. "You look surprised."

I blinked. "No, it's just … in high school, you were on top of the world. I never would have imagined you wanted it to be different."

"I didn't then, but I do now. I was such a cocky asshole."

We both chuckled.

"Don't fall over yourself disagreeing with me," he said, laughing louder. "Blowing out my knee may have been the best thing that could've happened. The demand and the pace of the pros were killing me, but I was too proud to walk away on my own. Thought it was all I had."

He took a deep breath. "I had a major lesson in humility, starting again with college. I may have drank more than I'm proud of. My wife and I considered separating. It's a damn miracle she stayed. I've always worshipped the ground she walked on but didn't show it. Now I'm all *date nights,* and *I'll take the kids* and pulling her out of my favorite dress about five minutes after she puts it on." He grinned, and now I envied him for something else. An image of

Hannah in that nightgown I'd never actually seen her wear popped behind my eyes.

We fell into easy conversation as I ran him through the workout and made a few notes for Tasha.

"Good to see you're doing well, man. Nice guy like you deserves it," Reid said.

"Ahh, but nice guys finish last." I wrapped the long, thin ice pack around his knee. "I think I heard you say that once or twice."

"Again, high school me was a dumb asshole. Nice guys may not win every lap, but if you notice, they usually win the race. Or better yet, they realize there is no race. We're all just out there trying to make our way through."

His words stayed with me for hours and into the night. I'd been the nice guy with women, then the not-nice guy, and the relationships still ended. And then it hit me.

Since Jessica, I'd played a role with women, and they knew it. I probably acted like a closed-off asshole. No wonder those relationships fizzled. But being truly open and vulnerable again, after what she did was tough stuff.

Except with Hannah. She'd made it easy.

We hadn't ended. I'd walked away. And I did it without even trying to fight. That ache in my chest grew.

Finally, giving up on sleep, I flipped on ESPN in the pre-dawn hours Sunday morning. They were broadcasting the final Formula One race of the season from Abu Dhabi. The announcers had droned on about the *amazing newcomer* to the grid who drove for Jaguar. I'd been glued to the coverage as they listed his stats and speculated about how he would be one of the greats like Hamilton, Schumacher, and Vettel.

I'm sure he was awesome, but would he love Hannah and the baby more than racing? Would he love them more than I did? No one could love them more than I did.

What if Reid was right, and the nice guy didn't finish last? What would happen if I told her I didn't want just a weekend? I wanted her and Bump forever. And I would fight anyone, even the god-like Lorenzo Messina, to have them.

21

HANNAH

For the first time in more than a year, I was in my office in late November, and I was warm. No need to storm into Grant's office and demand he turn up the heat. The disappointment was heavy.

A while ago I heard his door open and close but I hadn't seen him yet. I missed him.

I'd spent the rest of the weekend thinking about our time together in Las Vegas and here in Bend. Over the past year, I'd anticipate seeing him at work, wondering what he would do to annoy me, if his beard had any more gray in it, or if he would smell freshly showered from his workout. Even arguing, he made the days better because he challenged me and rarely backed down. He admitted when he was wrong but didn't pull any punches when he was right. And he made sure I got the ten-pack of blue Pilot gel pens in the holiday gift exchange last year. That thought made me grin.

God, I loved him. If Bethany was right, and he loved me back, I would have the dream I never believed possible.

I'd practiced a million conversations with him, but there was only one way to do this. He and I didn't hold back. Raw honesty was how this worked. I would tell him how I felt and that I wanted him for me *and* the baby. I'd take him to coffee or something away from campus, put it all on the table … and pray he felt the same.

Grabbing my laptop with my lecture notes, I opened my office door and almost bumped into the man. "Grant," I said as the blush rose with my nerves. I struggled to swallow at the sight of his golden eyes and wonderfully delicious lips.

"Hannah," he said, his voice like velvet. "You look beautiful. How was your Thanksgiving?"

"Good, you?" I shifted on my feet, searching for something to say like I was a teenager in prom season standing in front of the cutest boy in school. Well, I was standing in front of the hottest *man* in school.

To add emphasis to my point, two students walked by with eager expressions. "Hi, Professor Robolin," one girl said. "How was the conference?"

Grant looked over, startled by the question. "Oh, fine. Thank you, Stacy."

Stacy rolled her glossy lips and smiled a little too brightly. "Good … see you in class."

"See you then," he said and turned back to me. "Don't say it."

I bit my lip, and the familiar fire blazed in his eyes while a heaviness settled in my core. He stared at my mouth. That had to be a good sign. Right?

It was a heady experience, standing here with this provocative man and imagining the life we'd build together. A house in a neighborhood, birthday parties at home, and dinner at the table. Not nannies and benefits and phone calls from across the world.

I wanted him. I wanted to pull him close in front of all those pretty undergrads, male and female. They probably assumed the nerdy stats teacher had no game. What a surprise it would be to watch *me* get the sexy professor everyone wanted. Eat your heart out mean girls from high school.

My plan to take him for coffee flew out the window. Like always when I was with Grant, I couldn't control my blurting. "Grant, I …" Shit. I pulled him inside the doorway of my office. "Grant, I …" You want something, ask for it. "I don't want just a weekend. I want us to keep seeing each other, to see where this goes." I chewed the inside of my lip and breathed in. "I'll fly up to see you and fly you down to see me as much as we want." I lowered my voice. "You know I have access to at least one private plane."

He blinked and met my gaze with a simple nod, his expression serious.

"Do you want to keep seeing *me*?" I asked, my heart hovering somewhere in the vicinity of my throat.

"What about … the father? You saw him again?"

"I did. Nothing's changed from what I told you last weekend. We met with our attorneys and started the paperwork for him to give up his rights. It won't be final until it goes before the judge after the baby is born, but he signed. She's *mine*."

"I can't believe he doesn't want you, Hannah. What if he changes his mind?"

"It's too late for that, and he doesn't want me. But more importantly, I don't want him. I want you, for more than a night or a weekend, more than a couple of weeks. I …" Those three little words hung between us, but I didn't say them. "I want to do this with *you*."

He said nothing.

"Professor Byrne? Cooper and Naveen are downstairs. We're reviewing the analysis for our final project, and something isn't right. Could you take a look before class? We're freaking out a little."

I stared at the student standing just outside the office door and rapidly firing words at me. My brain caught up. "Of course, Madison," I replied, then looked at Grant. His face was unreadable. "This class is an hour. Will you be in your office after?"

He nodded but still said nothing. I turned to the stairs. We needed more time to talk about this. Me and my stupid blurting were fucking this up.

"Hannah …" Grant said.

I spun back to face him. His lips parted then closed.

"An hour. I'll be back in an hour. Think about what I said." My hands shook as I gripped my laptop tighter and walked down the hall.

I was a few steps behind Madison as I descended the modern floating staircase in the center of the large open lobby of the sciences building. Two huge skylights above bathed the entire space in soft winter sunlight that glinted off the brushed steel of the thick handrail.

A small circle of my students sat off to the side in a cluster of low-back sofas with spiral notebooks and laptops littering the table in the middle. I set my computer on the edge, inhaled deeply, and tried to slow the hammering of my heartbeat.

"Show me what you have," I said.

Naveen stepped closer with his laptop open.

"Hannah!" I twisted to see Grant leaping down the stairs two at a time, swinging around the mid-rise landing with the precision of a race car.

"Imperfect data, right?" he called, and I furrowed my

brow. "Data can be imperfect, you said. Statistics help us find the truth with imperfect data."

I stared at him, puzzled at his words, but my heart started thumping again. "Grant um … Professor Robolin." I glanced at all the wide-eyed students' rapt attention as he approached. When he captured my gaze, his held an intensity I hadn't seen before. Well, except for a few times last weekend when he was about to make me lose my mind in the best way.

"I know about imperfect data." He stopped in front of me close enough for me to inhale a hit of his familiar clean scent. "See, I believed only assholes got the girl. Not the nice guy. All the data I collected confirmed it. However, my research design was flawed. I was collecting data on the wrong women. Women I wasn't truly myself with. Then there you were, the perfect woman I could be real with, *nice* with. The corrected design yielded more accurate results. The answer was there all along."

He brushed his fingertips across my cheek, and I swear I heard at least three students swoon. A slow curve shaped his full lips, and I exhaled. "Grant, what are you—"

"I love you, Hannah."

"Grant …" I wrapped my arms around his neck and breathed him in. He pulled me tight to his chest, and I felt his heartbeat thumping wildly in the same rhythm as mine. "I love you too."

I pulled back and stared into his warm and wonderful eyes. "I love you so fucking much." He grinned, and I grinned, and then I kissed him with mindless abandon. Fortunately, he still had the self-awareness to refrain from too much tongue and ended the kiss as the swoons and whistles grew in decibels.

He pulled away, and his focus slid to the slightly larger

bump between us. He pressed his lips against my ear as the blood rushed through my veins. "I want you, and I want her. Let *me* be her dad, and I promise I'll love you both with everything I am."

22

GRANT

"I miss the Vegas heat," Hannah grumbled and shuddered as we stepped into the warmth of The Boathouse bar in Perry Harbor. The wind off the nearby water had a bite to it.

"We'll find family-friendly tropical locations for midwinter trips." I grinned.

"That's a few days. How will I ever keep warm the rest of the time?" Her eyes held a teasing gleam.

"I'll find a way." I waggled my eyebrows.

"Promises promises."

"Oh, I'll keep my promises. You know I will." I bent to kiss her delicious, if chilly, lips.

The last two weeks of the semester had flown by with finals and practical exams during the day and Hannah and I together every night. Usually, we stayed in Hannah's third-floor loft in an old building near the shopping district. It was your average industrial chic loft space, but Hud had the place wired for security. It even had a panic room. She wanted to live normally, but I respected the process that kept her safe.

She went to California, and I went to Washington after finals like we'd planned. I familiarized myself with Perry Harbor and the housing market. She and her mom started making all the baby plans. Then, I spent Christmas with her family at what I can only describe as a compound. Her famous parents, though guarded, were welcoming. I didn't push. I loved Hannah, and they loved Hannah. That's all that mattered. We'd figure the rest out in time.

Now, she was in Perry Harbor to meet my family, and I had a surprise in my pocket that I hoped to slip on her finger at midnight.

We were early, but the place was already filling up. A popular hangout for locals and tourists alike, The Boathouse atmosphere was warm and inviting, with exposed brick walls, dark wood tables, and a long copper-topped bar. Sinatra-style Christmas carols played low in the background. Colorful lights wound around a couple of wooden boats suspended from the ceiling. And Happy New Year streamers hung in the windows, preparation for tonight's celebration.

Hannah took in the open space. "Did you make a reservation?"

"Mom did." I didn't see a hostess. "Let's check with the bartender."

With her hand in mine, I led us between a group of tables to the bar.

"Grant." I swiveled to find Nicole Freeman, a family friend.

"Nicole. How are you? This is my girlfriend, Hannah." I pulled her close, and the two women shook hands. "Nicole used to live in the apartment behind my mom's old house. She helped to keep an eye on things. Gave David and me peace of mind knowing she was there." I turned back to Nicole. "I hope your new place is working out."

Nicole smiled and glanced at the muscular bartender hovering nearby. "Yep. It is. Grant, this is my boyfriend, Rhys. Rhys, this is Ms. Robolin's younger son, Grant."

Rhys gave me a pleasant head tilt from behind the bar. "What can I get you?"

"We have a reservation. Robolin. Party of five … for an early dinner."

"Oh, right. She just called to confirm. Let me get Sadie, and we'll get you seated."

"Celebrating the new year Perry Harbor style?" Nicole asked.

"If that means dinner with family and an early bedtime." Hannah casually put her hand on Bump and glanced at me.

"Whatever you need, baby."

Settled in a large booth near the back, we scanned the menu.

"They have some interesting mocktails," she said. "I may never leave."

Yeah, that was sort of the plan.

Emily said Hannah wanted to move to a small town after the baby was born. I wanted Perry Harbor to be that small town. David had asked me to help get the satellite office off the ground but left the end date open. I'd never imagined wanting to live in a small town again when I couldn't get out of the one where I grew up fast enough. I needed more than bonfires, high school sports, and grown-ass adults getting into fistfights about an umpire's call at the little league game.

This small coastal town was different. There were summer concerts in the waterfront park, a community theater, and miles of hiking and biking trails. The local hospital had access to some of the best doctors on the West Coast. Strangers smiled when they passed on the sidewalk, and the downtown area was busy with shops and restaurants. Small, well-kept houses lined the streets on the harbor side of the island, and the views were spectacular.

"GRANT, THIS IS BEAUTIFUL," Hannah said with a shiver, stepping into the rustic cabin at Anna Island Resort, a seaside retreat right across the channel from Perry Harbor. The wind directly off the water was damp with the light rain, and Hannah clutched the two plush throw blankets she'd brought—the woman traveled with about a dozen of them.

I spied the woodstove and the stack of split cedar logs next to it. "Let me set these things down, and I'll build you a fire. Two minutes, baby." I dropped our overnight bags on the king-sized bed and noticed the private hot tub on the back deck. Another time, after the baby arrived, we'd come back and enjoy that. Already looking forward to it, I rolled the small cooler of supplies over to the kitchenette area.

She arrived yesterday, joining me at my A-frame rental house only a few steps from the island's rocky shore. Winter wasn't the high season here, and I'd scored a great rental while I house-hunted. I'd planned to sell my condo in Bend and buy in Perry Harbor, but I hoped Hannah and I would be house hunting together after tonight.

Since it was New Year's Eve, I'd planned something special for tonight. Tess and her man Drew owned this cozy resort on neighboring Anna Island. She'd told us all about it in Vegas, and I'd pictured coming here with Hannah too many times. Tonight, we were spending the night in one of the treehouse cabins, Tess called them, which were built into the hillside and nestled into the surrounding old-growth Douglas firs.

"It does feel like a treehouse." Hannah stared with glittering eyes as she took in the warm space. "And this bathroom is amazing," she said, peeking inside. "The steam shower is already calling my name." I chuckled as I unloaded the snacks, breakfast foods, and sparkling cider I brought.

"We have all night, baby. Take a shower while I start the fire."

She went to her bag and unpacked enough to find her toiletry case, and I caught sight of the nightgown we bought in the maternity shop in Vegas. I'd finally seen her in it our first night together in Bend. She looked too damn sexy. The deep royal blue made her eyes glow, and the stretchy fabric hugged every curve, including her fuller breasts and growing bump. Fuck, I loved seeing her in that thing. And out of it.

"How about you start the fire and join me in the shower. I know it's one of your favorites." Her eyes were heavy with suggestion, and my dick thickened. It wasn't surprising. It had been almost an entire twenty-four hours since I was last buried deep inside her, the only place I truly wanted to be.

"Deal," I said and closed the lid of the empty cooler, then headed to the woodstove, trying not to be distracted by the sight of Hannah removing her shoes, then her bulky sweater and jeans. She sprinted to the bathroom in a blur of brown freckles and deep red hair and turned on the shower.

The fire snapped and popped as the kindling caught easily. I added several pieces of seasoned wood and closed the glass door. Stripping by the bed, I couldn't get naked fast enough.

Hannah was already in the shower, with clouds of steam rising around her as she washed her hair. She was gorgeous. I loved her, and I wanted to marry her as soon as possible. I'd have done it yesterday if I could.

I slid into the wide, double shower behind her and pulled her to me, her back to my front. My hand rested over Bump as I kissed that spot behind her ear. I loved that spot, possibly more than Hannah did. My dick swelled to full mast and nestled into her incredible round ass.

"Up against the wall?" she asked. Her OB had given us the go-ahead for sex with another slightly embarrassing and slightly flattering directive at me to be gentle. Which I'd heartily agreed to do while Hannah fought a blush.

"Nah, baby. Let me take care of you." I spun her to face me, placed her hand on the tile ledge to keep her steady, and sank to my knees.

AFTER SHE ROCKED my world on *her* knees, we finished the shower, dressed in thick bathrobes, and lounged on the sofa. She watched the fire. I watched my finger draw lazy circles over the soft skin and freckles on her thigh peeking out from the side of the robe. My mind whirred. I was really doing this.

I told myself a million times it was too soon. And a million and one times, I looked at Hannah, certain she was it for me. That wouldn't change. So, yes, I was really doing this.

Smoothing my hands over her rounded belly, I said, "I love you, Hannah, and I love Bump."

"We love you back," she said, placing her hand over mine.

Taking a deep breath, I shifted onto the floor, settling between her bent legs and looking up into her beautiful face. Her eyes filled with all the love, and my heart skipped a beat. This was Hannah.

"I want you."

Her lips curved in a coy smile. "You have me."

"No, I want *you*. Not your money or your family or whatever those other assholes thought was better than you. Nothing is better than you." I brushed my thumb over her cheek.

She sucked in a breath and sighed through her smile. "Grant …"

"I want this. I want marriage and a house. I want to be the dad to this baby and a few more if it's okay with you. I want to argue and make up and be nice." She chuckled. "I want to go to work and come home to you. I want to spend all our holidays together." Her eyes shimmered with what I hoped were happy tears.

"I know this thing between us has been fast. But you like fast. I think I like it too." I grinned. "Your life is complicated, but I'll sign a prenup, an NDA, and whatever else your family's lawyer wants me to sign. I don't care. I just want you, Hannah. Will you marry me?"

23

GRANT

She said yes, and I'd slipped the diamond and platinum heirloom engagement ring onto her finger. Now, it glittered from a chain around her neck, along with a matching wedding band.

"Squeeze my hand as hard as you want, baby. I can take it." Hannah practiced the breathing exercises we learned in our birthing classes. "The anesthesiologist is on her way. Soon, you can have the epidural. You're doing great."

She breathed out, and the monitor showed that the contraction was subsiding. "Whew, it hurts like a mofo." She looked at Aurora, the nurse, who'd been by her side the last few hours. "My father is a billionaire. Isn't there some sort of special process for us entitled moms to help move this along?"

I chuckled. *I'll take things I never thought I'd hear Hannah say for 300, Alex.*

Aurora, who had to be in her late fifties, huffed, her brown eyes assessing. "I don't think so, honey. Childbirth is the great equalizer. That baby doesn't care who her grand-father is. She's in charge now, and you better get used to it." Her stern expression broke into a wide grin of ruby lips and round dark cheeks. She softened her voice and patted Hannah's hand. "It won't be much longer. Hang in there, girl. You got this."

Hannah exhaled. "I had to try."

"I get it. I've heard worse, believe me." She winked.

Another contraction hit hard as the doctor poked her head in the door. "Did someone call for an epidural?"

"Yes, here," Hannah grunted as if there was a question.

Soon, she lay on her side, resting more comfortably, and Aurora slipped out to update our families in a nearby private conference room. In the quiet, the world outside Perry Harbor's Harborland Hospital was dark except for the glittering lights of an oil tanker docked at the refinery across the bay.

I smoothed a hand through her short hair, then pressed my lips to her head. God, I loved this woman. "Get some rest, baby." I kissed her and slid my palm tenderly to Bump. "You too. We'll be here when you're ready."

Hannah made a small purring sound, pulled our joined hands under her cheek, and settled in.

Hannah

"She did it. I think she got it. Yes!" I pumped my fist gently at my side so I wouldn't disturb Libby, who had finally latched on to nurse without the lactation specialist shoving my breast in her mouth. Make no mistake. Breastfeeding was hard. Worth it. But hard.

All those pictures of moms with angelic little babies

happily suckling? Not in my world. Maybe someday, but not today. It wasn't just childbirth, but children that were the great equalizer. I had all the comforts money could buy, but breastfeeding was up to me and Libby alone.

Elizabeth Ruth Robolin was born one week after her due date and entered the world with fiery red hair and a fierier disposition. Grant fell in love instantly.

"You are superwoman, baby," he said, entering the family room with another enormous flower delivery. We'd been home three days, and the space already had several other arrangements. One from my parents, one from Bethany and Jon, and one from the Robolins—his mom, Ruth, his brother David, Lauren, and the kids. Several boxes and other deliveries littered the floor. We'd get there. We had more important things to do right now.

"Who are those from?"

Grant placed the arrangement on a table near the others and checked the card. "Lorenzo. It says *Congratulations to Elizabeth for getting the absolute best mom and dad*."

Everything was settled with the paternity paperwork. Grant had already started the adoption process as well, but we had to wait for this little firecracker to enter the world first. Lorenzo was open to occasional updates, and Libby learning his role in her life if she wanted that someday, but she was Grant's daughter. At the last meeting with the attorneys, he'd been somber when he said Grant was the dad and always would be.

The man hovered above, smitten as any father could be. On our first day home, my heart swelled at seeing them together. Her tiny body dressed in that Formula One onesie curled into the crook of his muscular arm, and her tiny mouth puckered like a kiss as she slept. He never stood a chance. None of us did.

I smiled up at him. "I couldn't do this without you, you know."

He pulled my hand to his lips and kissed above the platinum band and the diamond ring he'd placed there. "I love you, Hannah."

We'd had a beautifully intimate wedding in the shadow of the red rocks outside Las Vegas on Valentine's Day. Our families and a few friends stood nearby, cheered, and never said a word about how my white dress framed my very pregnant belly like it was designed that way. Actually, it had been. I wanted Libby to be highlighted in the pictures as much as Grant and me. She was what brought me to Vegas. She was what finally brought us together, and I would be forever grateful.

A month later, we received the keys to a house on the west side of the island. Teams of people had worked to remodel it from a stark fortress behind wrought iron to something brighter, warmer, and more like a home. Not quite the picket fence of my dreams, but the new modern electronic gate was close enough. The house sat above a low cliff, up from a small cul-de-sac of similar gated homes rumored to throw fun add-a-dish dinners in the summer.

Hud supervised the installation of the security system and hired personnel. Decorators decorated. Housekeepers cleaned. Cooks cooked. Finally, it was me, Grant, and our baby girl in the private wing of our house.

Bliss-filled times were ahead. However, at this moment, I hadn't showered in days. My short hair was one nap away from being hopelessly matted. And I hadn't moved from my spot on the world's most comfortable sofa except to pee and go to bed. I lived in yoga pants and went topless most of the time because I was always breastfeeding or recovering from breastfeeding.

Grant said he liked the topless part, and I did, too,

because he joined me. He said it was because he kept the heat up, but it was actually to allow skin-to-skin contact with our daughter when he held her. Turns out we were a topless family most days. But then we were the product of one extraordinary weekend in Vegas, so it fit. We were a Vegas family: me, Grant, and our Vegas baby.

EPILOGUE

Hannah

"Would you like ice?" I spun from filling a glass at the fridge to the beefy security guard standing next to Hud in the kitchen of the private wing.

"No, thank you," he said, shifting his weight slightly.

"We're glad you're here," I said as I handed him the water, then tried to grin at the older man who was a fixture in my life … until now.

"Mommy!" Libby called down the hall from the main entrance. "We saw otters! They played and swam just like they do on the rocks in the park," she announced, entering the sunny room.

Peter, our two-year-old German Shepard rescue, trotted behind her, ever vigilant in monitoring his charge anytime she was in his presence. We hadn't trained him as a guard dog. He'd assumed the role on his own.

Libby stopped with a cautious start, and Peter promptly sat next to her with a thump, close enough for her to feel his thick fur through her colorful tights and favorite summer dress. "Hello. I'm Elizabeth Ruth Robolin, and this is my dog, Peter. We live here. What's your name?"

"Libby—" I started.

"Steve … Steve Hudson." The man kept his face blank as he took in the ice cream stain down the front of her and the mismatched shoes. Libby chose them on purpose, expressing her individuality. "You can call me Hud if you like."

"We already have a Hud. And a Peter." She said, gesturing to the dog still sitting like a sentinel beside her. The expression on his doggie face was pleasantly guarded. Yes, our dog had expressions, and they were surprisingly easy to read.

"Peter is named after the dog in *Peter Pan*. Do you know the story?"

"I do. Why didn't you name the dog Nana, like the dog in the story?" He asked plainly.

"Peter didn't like it. He liked Peter," she said, putting an end to further explanation. "We could call *you* Nana."

Hud let a small smile slip through his gray whiskers as the younger man cleared his throat. "No, I don't like that name for me either."

"I think you should call him Hud," the original Hud stood from a bar-height stool and moved closer to Libby. Peter relaxed his doggie expression at the approach of the man he must have seen as his partner in the important job of keeping Libby safe.

"But when I call for you, how will you tell which one I want?" Her little brow furrowed with the reasonable question.

He crouched low and gently took one of her hands in his. "He'll be the only Hud able to hear it, Little Miss. I won't be working here anymore. This is my nephew, and he's going to take over for me."

Libby cautiously returned her gaze to Steve, taking in the black T-shirt and pants, the buzz-cut hair, and tanned skin. My heart broke at the questions stirring right below the surface.

"I'm retiring," Hud explained. "Like your grandpa is retired."

"Are you going to go around the world in your big boat like my grandpa?"

Hud bit his lip and grinned. I'd only seen the endearing expression since Libby was born. "Possibly. I met a nice woman. She has a boat, and she'd like me to go with her on a trip. The boat's not as big as your grandpa's, but there's enough room for the two of us."

"Is there room for me? Could I come visit your boat?"

Hud considered her question as my heart swelled. I'd known Hud practically since I was Libby's age. He was family, and honestly, the little girl inside me wanted to ask to go too.

"I think there's just enough room for you. We could take a cruise to some of the islands."

"Oh, can we go to Lopez Island? It's gots lots of ice cream. I love ice cream."

Hud chuckled. "I know, Little Miss." He tugged on the hem of her skirt where the chocolate stain ended. "I think we can arrange that if your mom and dad say it's okay. You are a lot like your mom. Did you know that?"

"Yes." She raised her chin and smoothed what was probably a sticky hand through her curls. "My daddy says I'm smart and pretty like her."

I fought the threatening tears as Grant strolled in, carrying Libby's backpack. I grinned at him with his shirt wrinkled, his hair mussed, and a smaller version of the same ice cream stain on his shoulder. "How was the preschool field trip, Mr. Chaperone?" I chuckled. "You look …"

"Handsome and manly?"

"I was going to say tired."

He sucked in air. "Yeah, I'm that." He glanced around the somber room and frowned. "What'd I miss?"

Grant

I was happy to be one of several parent volunteers for the preschool's big summer field trip to the Seattle Aquarium. A beautiful sunny day with funny animals, sticky foods by the water, and two dozen three-year-olds running amok. What could go wrong?

"Hud came to say goodbye," Hannah said, surreptitiously wiping a tear. "But he invited Libby for a cruise on the boat with him and his friend sometime soon."

"No one she'd be safer with." I nodded at the man who meant a lot to me because he meant the world to my two favorite women.

Hud was retiring. It had all been planned, and his nephew Steve was stepping into some huge shoes. Hud said it would be a seamless transition, and I trusted him. The hitch was Libby.

Her gaze moved from Hud, who squatted before her, to me. Peter's watchful guard-dog eyes did the same. Libby's held so much trust and worry she wanted me to ease. My breath still caught sometimes at the reality that she was *my* little girl, and her incredible mom was my wife.

I let the small green Tinker Bell backpack slide down my arm as I crouched low to meet her gaze. "I know you'll miss Hud, sweetie. We all will. And he'll miss us. But now it's time for him to play and not work anymore. He'll get to have weekend-fun-days every day. Won't that be great?"

Her expression was still sad as the springy red curls bounced with her agreement. "He said I should call the new man Hud."

"That sounds good to me. It might even help us remember our friend." She nodded again, more emphatically this time, and then fell into the arms of the first Hud. I glanced at Hannah, her hand over her mouth and another shimmer of tears at the edges of her eyes.

The love in this room was palpable. This woman and all her life and light, this little girl. I hit the jackpot in Vegas.

"Is she down?" I asked as Hannah ambled into our bedroom in a silky robe I hoped hid something lacy and easily removable underneath.

"She is." Hannah sighed and sat on the bed. "New Hud helped us coordinate calendars for a boating afternoon with Old Hud, and I think the process helped. Peter's still not sure about the change, so he's staying extra close to Libby. But his doggie face looks a little less serious."

"She had a big day."

Hannah laid on the pillow propped next to mine and nudged my leg with her hand. "She's not the only one. I'm surprised you're still awake after that field trip."

"Sea lions, otters, and sharks, oh my!" I sang like Dorothy and the Scarecrow on the yellow brick road.

"It's part of the dad gig. Maybe I should have warned you, but it's too late now. The papers are legally binding. You're locked in." She rolled on top of me and settled exactly the way I liked. She knew me well. My dick instantly thickened. "Is the dad gig still working out for you?"

Hannah sometimes asked the question with apprehension. Babies can be a challenge, and Libby was no exception. Diapers and sleepless nights were only the beginning. But dads showed up for the good stuff and the bad. And I was the dad.

I rolled us both until I was over her and pressed my now fully hard dick against her center. "Yes, the dad gig and the husband gig, and even the son-in-law of a famous billionaire gig. It's all working out for me, better than I could've imagined."

"Good," she said. "Because you weren't the only one who had a big day today. Our little project had a big day too."

I paused. Hannah and I had been trying for another baby for about a year with no success. *Secondary infertility*, the doctors called it. We both had all the tests, and they assured us everything looked good. It would just take time. Was she saying what I thought she was saying?

Hannah met my eyes with a coy expression, and my heart thumped. "I'm pregnant, and you're the father," she stated, her tone pragmatic and so much the sexy statistics professor I loved.

"Really?" I couldn't hide my happy.

"Yes, I'm pretty sure it's yours," she teased, her face glowing.

"Oh, she's mine. *I'm* the motherfucking dad." I waggled my brows, and Hannah giggled at my choice of words. Quickly, I kissed her lips before blazing a trail lower, between her soft breasts and down to her belly. "I love you, Hannah." I kissed her still-flat stomach through the silky robe, already picturing it growing. "And I love you too, baby."

"We love you back," she said.

"You wanna … take a little trip to celebrate?" I matched her smile with my own, ideas pinging in my head.

Her eyes glittered. "Any specific place you had in mind?"

"Hmmm," I said, acting as if I was deep in thought. "How 'bout Vegas?"

Thank you for reading *Vegas Baby*! I hope you loved Grant and Hannah's journey to happily ever after. If you did, please leave a review where you purchased the book, or on Goodreads or Bookbub to help other readers find characters and stories they will love.

Ready for more steamy stories with all the feels? Grab bonus scenes and more on my website at www.christinabraver.com/bonus/.

And grab ***Formula One Noel*** (Walker & Nora) for more Formula One and the holidays. (Walker is Hannah's friend and the former F1 driver Lorenzo replaced on Team Jag. His road to an HEA with Dr. Nora Reynolds is not to be missed.)

Two overachievers. One incredible night. Can they add up to forever?

Dr. Nora Reynolds saves lives. It's what she does. It's all that matters.

Walker Hewitt wins Formula One races. It's what he does. It's all that matters.

She's on the verge of leaving the ER to do research despite her parents' objections. He's on the verge of leaving the flashy career his billionaire family is so proud of. They both need a break. A snowstorm trapping the two strangers in the city is the perfect opportunity to be someone else for a while.

It's one blissful night against a backdrop of holiday lights. Until Walker invites Nora to spend a few more days with him on his family's snowy private island off the Washington coast. They'll be alone. She can work on her grant proposal by day, and he can worship her body by night. It's perfect.

But a glimpse of life with Walker threatens Nora's resolve to keep it casual. It was just supposed to be one night. Now he wants them all. She could never abandon her life's work to follow her heart … could she?

A STEAMY, forced proximity, secret identity, he falls first, billionaire love story containing a driven heroine, a racy hero, and a touch of holiday magic. It's about performance, family, and the lies we believe until love makes the truth impossible to ignore.

WANT to know more about Hannah's sister Bethany, Perry Harbor, and the resort where Grant proposed?

Grab ***Your Heart*** (Drew & Tess) today! This is Book 3 in the Perry Harbor series, but all books can be read as standalones.

PERRY HARBOR IS a close-knit small town nestled in the San Juan Islands north of Seattle. Beauty. Family. Future. Close friends and big loves challenge the residents and inspire us all.

. . .

A LITTLE BIT NERDY, and a little bit dirty, these books are steamy and deal with deeper issues like women's health and sex positivity for all genders. Low angst with all the feels and a swoony HEA. No cheating and no cliff-hangers.

WANT the inside scoop on my misadventures in writing along with freebies and real sex positive info from my reading and research? Sign-up for my newsletter via my website:

www.christinabraver.com. Unsubscribe at anytime.

As MUCH AS I TRY, I'm not perfect. If you find an error, please email me at:

author@christinabraver.com.

ALSO BY CHRISTINA BRAVER

Want more stories about independent women making their way in the world and the sexy men who fall hard for them?

Scan the QR code below for the full list of Christina Braver novels. Or head to the Books page of my website, christinabraver.com.

ChristinaBraver.com Books Page

ACKNOWLEDGMENTS

Thank you to all the wonderful people who made this story possible.

To Ann B., Julie F., Kim S., Maryanne K., Melissa B., and Serena B., my beautiful book betas who bravely read this manuscript first.

To Brent Archer, my fabulous writing sprint partner who helps me plot and keeps me writing.

To my Editor, Lynne, for her continuous support, making my books better and showing up at every event. I appreciate you.

To Reid K. and his team at Phenix, to Rebecca, Laurie, Karrin, and all the other pros who keep this writer's back healthy enough to keep writing. Special thanks to Reid K. for naming Grant and sharing his physical therapy expertise.

To all my friends, with or without glasses of wine, who have supported and encouraged me along this journey. You know who you are, and I know who you are. Thank you!

To my kids for supporting me, even with the embarrassment of having a mom who writes explicit stories.

To my husband and very own beta hero statistician who makes this work possible and first said the words "You should write a book."

ABOUT THE AUTHOR

Christina Braver writes steamy, small-town, contemporary romance usually set in the Pacific Northwest. Her stories are about strong heroes with softer sides, independent heroines with a bit of sass, and the guaranteed happily-ever-after we all need.

She has a master's degree in clinical psychology and uses that knowledge to create well rounded character driven stories described as "a little bit nerdy and a little bit dirty." Influenced by books and information from prominent sex therapists, her novels bring toe curling spice and real-life sexy tips, as well as address deeper issues such as women's sexual health and sex positivity for everyone.

She lives outside Seattle, and when she isn't writing, Christina can be found biking with her husband, laughing too loudly with friends, sipping wine, or reading.

www.ingramcontent.com/pod-product-compliance
Lightning Source LLC
Chambersburg PA
CBHW060325310726
48976CB00007B/2451